LOVE AFTER... LOVE

A GETAWAYS NOVELLA

HARPER ROBSON

2024

Cover Design by Natasha Snow at Natasha Snow Designs

Editing by Sandra and Julia at One Love Editing

Backmatter Updated: May 19, 2025

Love After Love

Getaways Book Two: A Novella

Jesse

After my ex's betrayal, I swore off love forever.

Then Martin Benoit landed in my life, with his silver hair and Irish charm. Now we're roommates and business partners, and I'm fighting a losing battle against my feelings.

Martin

I've been alone since losing the love of my life 25 years ago, convinced my heart was closed for good.

But Jesse Greenwood, with his warm heart and genuine optimism, makes me question everything I thought I knew.

He makes me feel like second chances might be possible after all.

But am I brave enough to risk it all again?

From Disneyland adventures to moonlit beach walks, this steamy, age-gap romance proves it's never too late for a second chance at love--if you're brave enough to take the leap.

Author's Note

Love After Love was originally published as part of the Summer Nights Prolific Works Giveaway in August, 2024. It has been further edited and expanded by more than 8,000 words.

I hope you enjoy Jesse & Martin's story!

Contents

Prologue

Jesse

Okay, so if I'm completely honest, coming to the grand opening party at *The Open Door* tonight would not have been my first choice. I'd much rather be at home, alone, drowning my sorrows and searching for answers at the bottom of a bottle.

Instead, I'm standing alone in the middle of this happy crowd, nursing my second—or is it my third?—drink of the night as joy and excitement radiate from every corner of the room. This shelter for LGBTQ youth in a town just north of Seattle is something my friends Penn and Hunter have been working on for several years, and I was lucky enough to get involved a couple of years ago. It's a huge accomplishment, and I'm thrilled for them.

Delighted, even.

Honestly.

The alcohol is helping. Or it was until Hunter gets down on one knee in front of Penn and pops the question. Yes. *That* question.

My stomach drops as the room erupts into cheers.

It's only been three days since I signed the final divorce papers, putting a sharp point on nearly two decades of my life. A couple of years of dating, fifteen years of marriage, plus two years of messy negotiations, heartache and shattered trust—all wrapped up in a neat little package of legalese.

But maybe their marriage will work out better than mine did. Of course, I thought mine would too, so what the hell do I know?

As grief claws at my chest like a ravenous beast, all I want to do is scream and shatter my almost empty—*and how did that happen?*—glass against the wall and storm off to lick my wounds in private.

But I can't. I won't.

Instead, I swallow the mountain-sized lump in my throat and raise my glass to toast the happy couple along with everyone else.

"Congratulations, you two," I tell them a few minutes later, hoping they don't notice my strained tone. I know I'm busted when Penn raises his eyebrow pointedly at me before crushing me in a huge hug.

A few minutes later, as I'm getting ready to slip away, hopefully unnoticed, Martin Benoit appears beside me. I'd wanted to chat with him earlier and run a few ideas past him about plans I have for a shelter similar to this at home in San Diego, but those good intentions are all buried under a big pile of grief and irritation at the moment.

"I recognize that look in your eye," he says, his soft Irish lilt curling around me. In another life, I'd find it attractive. I *have* found it attractive the few times we've chatted.

"Oh? What look is that?" I ask, signaling to the bartender for another round.

"The look of a man trying to decide how soon he can leave without being rude and then trying to decide whether he cares."

I snort. "That obvious?" I ask, nodding in appreciation when the bartender refills my sad little glass.

Martin shoots me a wink, his green eyes twinkling. "Come on, pal. Let me drive you back to your hotel. We've not had the chance to properly catch up tonight." He leans in with a conspiratorial whisper, "And I've been trying to make my own escape for the last twenty minutes."

Well, that sounds like an offer I can't refuse.

And that's how I find myself sitting across from Martin in the bar of my hotel, nursing a couple of fingers of Bushmills 21. At this point, I've lost count of how many I've had, but it doesn't seem to matter because the alcohol's done a shit job of dulling the pain in my chest.

"Thanks again for the ride," I say. "You really didn't have to. I know I'm terrible company right now."

He waves me off. "Not at all. Like I said, we didn't get a chance to catch up during the party. Plus, you looked like you could use a friend and maybe another wee dram," he says, holding up his own glass with a mischievous smile. "For medicinal purposes, naturally."

Martin is a consultant Penn worked with to plan and build *The Open Door*. I spent a lot of time in Seattle during the project, but most of it was during off-hours when I wasn't busy running the green energy company I own with my brother. As a result, I didn't spend much time with the handsome Irishman, although I've always thought he seemed like a good guy.

I don't know if it's the alcohol, the atmosphere, or my melancholy mood, but the smooth lilt of his voice is sending shivers down my spine, and the way the laugh lines crinkle around his green eyes when he smiles causes a pool of liquid heat to settle down low in my belly.

I let my eyes drift over him. He must be in his mid-fifties, shorter than me, with a solid, compact build. He has thick, wavy hair and just enough stubble to feel incredible against my skin. It's entirely possible the term "silver fox" was coined specifically for this man.

Martin blinks at me and cocks his head to the side, jolting me back into reality.

My therapist assures me that my current lack of focus is just my depression, and I'm not actually losing my damn mind. Sometimes, I'm not so sure.

I clear my throat. "Um, I'm sorry, what was that?"

He chuckles, and there are those damn laugh lines again.

"I was just asking about your plans now that *The Open Door* is officially off the ground, but it looks as though you might've been in another dimension for the last few minutes."

I huff out an embarrassed laugh.

He pauses before speaking, his tone warm. "No pressure at all, but if you need an ear, I'm a decent listener."

I swirl the amber liquid in my glass. "I'll be okay." *Will I? Yes. Probably. Maybe.*

He doesn't respond, just looks at me over the rim of his glass as he takes a sip. For some reason—it could be the company or maybe it's my slow progression into a stupor—I keep talking.

"I'm happy for Penn and Hunter. Honestly, I am. It's just that... Well, I guess today wasn't the best day for me to be a witness to a romantic, public proposal. Not after I just signed the death certificate on my own happily ever after." I toss back the remainder of my drink and catch the bartender's eye, signaling for another. One more won't hurt. *At least not until tomorrow.*

Martin nods. "I understand. Of course you're happy for them. But that doesn't mean their lovey-doveyness doesn't sting like salt in your wounds. You're allowed to be angry."

He gets it. It's like he's just thrown me a life preserver. Like I've finally found someone who isn't uncomfortable with all the baggage I'm lugging around.

I don't know all the details of his past, but I know he's a widower who lost his partner to AIDS back in the nineties. So I guess he understands something about carting around buckets full of pain and rage.

He takes another sip of his drink and then darts his tongue out, licking off the last remnants of the whiskey.

I wonder what he tastes like.

Suddenly, my own drink isn't nearly as interesting as it was a moment ago.

Out of nowhere, my pulse speeds up, a shock of heat running through my veins. It's like someone flipped a switch inside me, and all I can think about is how much I want him. Want to taste those lips. That skin. Want my mouth on his neck, his jawline, that spot behind his ear. I want to suck marks onto his collarbone and trace the colorful tattoos on his forearm with my tongue.

Want isn't a strong enough word.

Need fits better.

I've always been the laid-back type, letting life lead the way and following along. It's easy and comfortable, but it's not always satisfying. I'm not usually the guy who takes charge— who takes something for *himself*—but this moment is already ticking down, already turning into one more damn thing in my rearview mirror, and I can't let that happen. Not while my heart is hammering in my ribcage, not while Martin is only an arm's length away. Not while this one person who might make me feel better, or at least feel *something*, is finishing his second drink and looking like he's about to call it a night.

I shove my chair back, grab my wallet from my pocket, and toss a handful of bills onto the table. My cheeks are hot, and the fire in my belly is pushing me to just goddamn well *take* what I want. *What I need.* Maybe for the first time in my life.

I run my hand nervously through my hair, ignoring the surprised look on Martin's face. Do I look a little crazy? Probably, but at this point I don't give a tiny rat's ass.

I take a deep breath. "Look, I don't know what the hell I'm doing here, but I'm going to say this anyway." Say what, exactly, I don't even really know until the words fall from my lips.

"I want you to come upstairs with me, Martin. I want you to come to my room and take me apart the way I've been dying for. I know you can do it. And before you protest that you're taking advantage of me, the fact is, yes, I'm a little drunk, but I'm nowhere near so drunk that I don't know what I'm doing. I want this. I want *you*. I need to feel something other than rage and fucking bitterness. I just want to feel good. One night, no strings. That's it."

His mouth drops open in shock.

No turning back now.

Martin blinks once. And again.

Well, fuck. I guess it was worth a shot. I'm about to apologize and attempt to blame the alcohol, even though I've just assured him that I'm not too drunk, when Martin nods. He swallows the last of his drink and gets to his feet, his eyes never leaving mine. "After you, then."

My heart races like a *Formula One* car as I lead Martin back to my room. I'm both terrified and thrilled after making such a bold move for the first time in my almost forty-five years. I'm shaking with adrenaline, but the rush of *wanting* someone again is overwhelming. I finally feel alive instead of feeling hollow and empty inside.

My hand shakes as I use the key card to let us in. As the door swings open I catch a glimpse of the mirror and barely recognize myself—hair disheveled, cheeks flushed, eyes wild. My whole body is burning with lust.

Martin looks nearly as wrecked as I feel. His face is flushed, and his hair is mussed from running his hands through it. His hungry expression, his green eyes burning with his own lust just fuels my determination.

I *need* this—*I need him.*

"Oh, god," I mutter, grabbing a two handfuls of his shirt and crashing my mouth onto his. The sound of the door slamming shut behind us only adds to the intense heat consuming me from the inside out.

I grab the sides of his face and push him up against the door while I delve my tongue into his mouth, tasting the spicy hint of whiskey as I explore every part of him I can reach.

He wraps his arms around me, gripping the back of my neck before sliding his hands into my hair and pulling hard enough to sting.

I *love* it.

I grab his hips, holding on to him tightly. Our kisses are long and deep, and I never want it to stop. I want to live in this moment forever, feeling only the sensations of his hard cock against mine, the hot skin of his back under my hands, and his spicy, woodsy scent filling my nose.

I wrench my mouth off his, panting as I stare into his eyes, which have darkened with desire.

Swallowing hard, I toss all my inhibitions to the wind and blurt out what I need from him. "I want to fuck you. But it won't be sweet or tender. I want to fuck you hard. Tell me now if that's not okay."

His expression turns wicked, his mouth turning up in a feral smile. "Do your worst. Take what you need from me. I've got you."

I swallow again at his words, my chest tightening. *Oh God.*

"Do you know the traffic light system?" he asks. "Safe words?"

I'm not overly familiar with the BDSM lifestyle, but I've read enough to know what he's talking about. "Yeah, I think so," I answer breathlessly. "If you say 'red', everything stops, no questions asked, 'yellow' means we need to stop or slow down and 'green' means everything is fine, keep going."

He nods, looking at me, his eyes piercing. "That's right. Remember either one of us can safe-word anytime for any reason. Are you alright with that?"

I nod again, licking my lips. "Yeah. What color are you right now?" I ask, and he cocks an eyebrow at me.

"Very, very green."

"Thank fuck," I mutter, crushing my mouth back down onto his as I pull his shirt free from his dress pants, tearing it open roughly. Buttons fly everywhere, but I don't give a shit, desperate to get to what's underneath.

I moan into his mouth as I explore the lean, hard planes of his chest. His skin is hot under my hands as I slide them over the taut muscles of his abdomen, loving the rough texture of his happy trail.

I pull him off the door and turn us, not breaking our kiss as I guide us deeper into the suite.

Once we're next to the bed, I tear my mouth off his, panting as I work open his pants. He sucks in a sharp breath when I shove my hand into his briefs, grasping his cock firmly and stroking it before letting go to push his pants down.

I lick my lips as he steps out of the crumpled trousers and stands naked before. I bite down on my lip, stifling a groan as I admire him. He's compact but lean, all hard muscle and chest hair. His heavy cock juts out proudly from a thatch of dark curls, straining toward me. God, he's like a wet dream.

I frantically tear off my own clothes and push him roughly onto the bed, following him down and covering his body with mine. I slam my mouth back down on his, tangling our tongues together.

I roll my hips against his, sliding my cock against his as I groan, loving how his hard length feels against mine. He grips my ass and lifts his hips off the bed to meet my thrusts.

"Jesus," I mutter between feverish kisses. "You feel so good."

Our mouths battle for control, tongues dueling and teeth nipping. His cock swells and a growl of need escapes me.

I finally force myself to pull away, tearing my mouth away from his, panting heavily. His eyes are heavy-lidded and full of lust.

I press hot, open-mouthed kisses down his neck, nipping at his pulse point before trailing lower, down his chest and across his pecs. I flick my tongue over a flat nipple before taking it into my mouth and biting down.

He sucks in a breath and grips my hair, tugging hard. I moan at the sharp pain mixed with pleasure before continuing lower, intent on tasting every inch of him.

Thankfully, there's a travel-sized bottle of lube I tossed into the drawer beside the bed last night after jerking off in an unsuccessful attempt to get a decent night's sleep. Martin watches me as I reach over and fumble in the drawer, his chest rising and falling rapidly.

"That's convenient," he quips with a little smile when I triumphantly produce the lube.

I grin at him. "Yeah, well I was a Boy Scout, after all. Always believe in being prepared."

He chuckles as I slick up my fingers, adding a generous amount to my aching cock before returning my attention to him.

I gently push his legs apart, my eyes locking with his as I slowly drag my fingers through his crease and then push one inside him. He sucks in a sharp breath, his body tensing for a moment before he relaxes as I work my finger in and out of his body. I add another, and he rocks down onto my hand, seeking more.

"Color?" I check in.

"Green," he rasps, his eyes finding mine. "So green."

I suck in a breath, my body burning up with lust. Taking his cock in my other hand, I stroke him as I add a third finger, twisting them inside him and aiming for his prostate. He whimpers, and his cock jumps when I hit the spot. He arches off the bed, his mouth falling open as he pants and moans, his legs falling open.

"Keep going, don't stop," he begs, his voice hoarse.

Hearing him so wrecked and desperate sends a spike of pure lust straight to my cock, and I groan again, my hips instinctively jerking forward. "Soon," I whisper, watching in rapture as his body seems to suck my fingers inside over and over again, desperate and hungry for everything I'm giving him.

"So good," I mutter.

"Fuck, Jesse, I need you. Now," his voice is desperate, and the sound of it nearly pushes me over the edge.

"Okay, baby. I've got you," I whisper before realizing something. "Shit, we need a condom," I mutter.

"In my wallet. My pants pocket," he rasps.

"Thank god," I breathe in relief before I slowly pull my fingers from him. I hustle to where his pants are lying on the floor, and hurriedly find what I'm seeking, tearing open the condom package with my teeth as I hurry back to the bed and knee walk into position back between his legs.

Martin's eyes flash, and he pushes himself up on his elbows, watching intently as I roll the condom on. My hands shake with anticipation as I add more lube to my cock.

"You're gorgeous like this," Martin whispers, his eyes trailing over me. "Rough and wild. I love it."

I lean down, taking his mouth in a searing kiss as I push my way inside him. His body opens for me immediately, his heat nearly making me come before I'm even all the way inside him. He moans into my mouth, wrapping his arms around me.

I still for a moment, seeking to let him adjust. I know I told him I wasn't going to go easy, but I don't want to hurt him. Even in my desperation I want this to be good for him as well. But then he surprises me, punching his hips up and forcing me deeper.

"You promised you'd go hard," he growls.

I groan, my cock twitching inside the tight sheath of his body. "Fuck," I gasp, pulling almost all the way out before slamming into him, hard.

He groans. "Yessss," he hisses, shoving his hips up against mine.

I set a brutal pace, pounding into his body as he moans, his fingers digging into my back.

I move one hand to his cock, pumping it roughly in time with my hips. "God, you're so fucking tight," I breathe, nipping at his neck as I keep thrusting, loving the way his body claws at mine, urging me on.

"Please," he moans, and my eyes snap to his. "Harder."

I bite back another groan as I increase the force of my thrusts, loving the desperate, wanton way he begs for more.

"Please," he nearly sobs, writhing under me, and I'm done for.

I slam into him hard. His head falls back as he cries out, his body tensing as his ass clenches around me.

"So. Fucking. Hot," I pant, watching his eyes roll back in his head while I pound into him, my hips a blur. "Take it," I snarl. "Yes. Take all of me. Fuck yes. It's all yours."

He arches off the bed, crying out, his body shuddering. The feel of his inner muscles contracting around my cock while his orgasm rips through him pulls me over the edge.

With one last brutal thrust, I come, my head falling forward. I swear to god, I see stars as I grip him tightly, shuddering as I unload into the condom deep inside his body.

I hold him against me, as our sweat-slick bodies slowly calm, our harsh breaths mingling as we each try to get our bearings.

"Jesus," I finally whisper, lifting my head to find his eyes.

Martin grins at me. "Was that what you needed?"

"Oh, fuck yes."

Chapter One

Martin

Four Months Later

Jesse's waiting for me in baggage claim at the San Diego airport, looking tanned and relaxed in shorts and a T-shirt. He waves when he spots me, a grin lighting up his handsome face. My heart squeezes in my chest as I make my way to him, rolling my suitcase behind me. He looks much healthier and happier than he did the last time I saw him in person.

When he got in touch with me a few weeks after our night together to ask whether I would consider moving to California to help him build a similar shelter to *The Open Door*, I jumped at the chance. But that was before I realized the impact that night had on me. I knew at the time it wasn't a regular hookup;

our connection was unlike anything I've experienced since I lost my partner more than twenty years ago. But I didn't figure on becoming borderline obsessed with him. It's been months now, and I've not been able to stop thinking about him. I'm concerned things are going to be awkward if I can't hide how much he's been occupying my mind.

I don't do relationships. Ever. Losing Richard gutted me so badly that I swore off romantic love forever, and I've never once regretted that choice. This strange obsession is making me a bit nervous, to tell the truth. But I committed to the job, and it's an amazing opportunity, so I can only hope things will settle down in my mind now that I'm here.

"You made it! Great to see you!" he exclaims, pulling me into a warm hug. I inhale his clean, citrusy scent, and my travel tension magically disappears.

"Good to see you too. Thanks for picking me up."

"Of course. I'm so glad you're here," he says, smiling warmly.

As Jesse loads my suitcase into his SUV, I suck in a lungful of the warm air. Palm trees line the street leading out of the airport, and lights from the ships in the bay twinkle as we pass by. It's late since the three-hour flight left after I finished my last official work day at *The Open Door.*

"Welcome to sunny San Diego!" he declares as he merges his SUV onto the interstate. "I can't wait to show you around."

"Happy to be here," I say, stifling a yawn. I'm used to moving a lot—it's how I've avoided attachments, romantic or otherwise, since Richard died. I never stay in one place for more than a couple of years, and saying goodbye to friends in each city every time I leave is draining. Leaving Seattle today was no different. I truly loved my time working closely with Penn, but I'm looking forward to this latest fresh start.

Jesse offered me his spare room until I can get properly settled in the area. I accepted, gratefully, but I'm wondering if that might not have been the best choice, given that I can't stop thinking about him. However, what's done is done at this point, and he does seem genuinely excited to host me.

Half an hour later, he pulls up in front of a small but stylish home in an older neighborhood just a couple of blocks from the ocean. The surrounding houses are a mix of beautifully remodeled older homes and more modern places. Jesse lives in one of the newer-looking, infill-style homes, and it's gorgeous, with huge picture windows and a crisp, white exterior.

"Welcome to my little slice of paradise." He grins. "Moonlight Beach, one of my favorite spots in the entire world, is just down the hill."

The distant sound of crashing waves and the salty tang in the air confirm the proximity to the shore as I get out of the car and follow him to the front door. Our hands brush as he hands me my suitcase, sending a jolt of electricity up my arm. *Goddammit.* My attraction to him clearly hasn't dimmed at all in the last few months.

"Follow me. I'll show you your room first," he says, leading me up a set of stairs. "I hope this works for you." His voice is warm as I take in the space—a good-sized bedroom furnished with a modern but comfortable-looking bed, dresser, and a small seating area with a flat-screen TV on the wall and a large, cozy chair and ottoman combination that looks perfect for curling up with a good book.

"It's perfect. Thank you, Jesse." I set my bag down and turn to face him, very aware of how close he's standing.

His eyes meet mine, a flicker of heat passing between us. His pupils dilate as he swallows hard before clearing his throat. "I know it's late, but can I offer you anything to eat or drink?"

I glance at the clock, noting it's almost midnight. "No, I'm great, thanks. I might have a quick shower to rinse off the airplane funk before crawling into bed though," I say with a smile.

"Of course. Just make yourself at home." He licks his lips. "If, um, there's anything you need, or... whatever... I'm just down the hall."

"I appreciate that. Thanks, Jesse."

"Of course. Sleep well." He lingers a moment longer, his gaze roaming over my face as if memorizing every detail. Then, with a soft smile, he turns and heads for his own room.

I close the door and lean against it, letting out a shaky breath. *Sweet, suffering Jaysus.* This is going to be even harder than I thought.

A few hours later, I wake to the tantalizing scent of bacon and coffee. For a moment, I'm disoriented, but then I remember—I'm in Jesse's house in San Diego.

Pulling on a T-shirt, I follow my nose downstairs to find him standing barefoot in front of the stove. He's wearing low-slung pajama bottoms and nothing else. The muscles in his back flex as he scrambles eggs in a large cast-iron pan, and my cock twitches in my own loose sleep pants. Quickly, I slide onto one of the barstools at the island, effectively concealing myself. *Christ, I need to get a grip.*

"Morning," I mumble, my voice rough with sleep.

Jesse turns, a bright smile lighting up his face. "Hey there, sleepyhead. Hope you're hungry."

The kitchen is warm and inviting, filled with morning sunlight. It's been years since anyone's cooked for me like this. A wave of contentment washes over me.

"Starving," I admit.

"Good. I thought I'd give you a real SoCal welcome, so I made us breakfast burritos. I hope you like Mexican food."

He sets a mug of steaming coffee in front of me before turning back to the stove, and I chuckle at the expression on the mug: *"What, and I cannot stress this enough, the actual fuck?"*

"Well, in truth, I can't say as I've ever had a breakfast burrito before," I say, and he gasps, his eyes going comically wide as he clutches his chest in mock horror.

"My god, you can't be serious? You've never had a breakfast burrito? Well, you'd better hold on to your balls, my good man, because mine are some of the best!"

I bark out a laugh. "I appreciate your confidence."

A few moments later, he slides a plate in front of me and watches expectantly as I pick up the burrito and take a bite. The flavors explode in my mouth: creamy eggs, crisp, salty bacon, spicy salsa, and a tortilla that practically melts in my mouth. "Holy shite, this is amazing," I say before shoving another bite into my mouth.

His eyes crinkle with pleasure. "Glad you approve."

"Approve? I might become addicted," I mumble, my mouth half-full.

"Did you sleep okay?" he asks, picking up his own burrito.

"Like the dead. That mattress is a dream."

We fall into easy conversation, our laughter mingling with the sound of crashing waves filtering in through the open window.

After breakfast, we take our coffee up to the rooftop patio, where we spend a few hours discussing plans for the shelter and community/job training center. By early afternoon, we're both ready for a break.

"I think I'm about done for today. What do you think?" Jesse asks, stretching his arms above his head. "We could walk down to Moonlight Beach."

I nod, grateful for the chance to clear my head. "Sounds perfect."

The sun is warm on my skin as we stroll down the hill toward the beach. I love how at ease Jesse seems here, his shoulders relaxed and a content smile playing on his lips.

"God, it's beautiful here," I murmur as we get to an overlook next to one of the iconic California lifeguard towers. The view nearly takes my breath away. Golden sand stretches for miles in both directions, kissed by gentle waves that shimmer in the afternoon sun. The Pacific Ocean is a mesmerizing tapestry of blues, from deep navy to vibrant turquoise. "It's almost too perfect to be real."

He smiles and sucks in a deep breath of the ocean air. "I agree. California's not like anywhere else."

He leads me down a set of wooden steps leading to the beach, and when we get to the bottom, we both kick off our shoes. The feel of the warm sand between my toes is delightful.

We amble along the beach as the setting sun paints the sky in hues of gold and pink, casting a magical glow over everything. The rhythmic crash of waves provides a soothing backdrop to our comfortable silence.

I sneak glances at Jesse. He seems lost in thought, a small smile playing on his lips. I can't help stealing glances at him as we walk, my eyes drawn to his profile like a magnet.

"I come here a lot to clear my head," he says softly. "The past two and a half years were rough, and I'm so grateful I had this place so close by. Some days, I'd come here two or three times in one day just to get out of the house. Something about the sound of the ocean always makes me feel more at peace."

"That makes sense," I say. "Coming here sounds like a pretty healthy coping mechanism."

I pause for a moment before asking one of the many questions that have been on my mind since our night together. "I hope you don't mind me asking, but how are you doing now that some time has passed? You seem much better than the last time I saw you."

He gives me a rueful smile before directing his gaze out to the ocean. "I'm a lot better, but I still have shitty days," he says, not looking at me. "The hardest thing is that I no longer trust my instincts, which isn't like me. I'm an entrepreneur, for god's sake, so being unsure about every move I make is a problem. Thankfully, my brother's been able to pick up my slack. If we weren't partners in *Greenwood Energy*, I'm not sure the company would have survived."

He lets out a sigh, still focused on the vast expanse of ocean beside us as we walk slowly on the packed sand, letting each wave just kiss our bare toes before it retreats back. "And it goes beyond work. My self-confidence is just one of the many casualties of my marriage. I still find it frustrating that I can't have a simple conversation the way I used to."

I cock my head to the side. "What do you mean by that?"

He stops, digging his toes into the cool, wet sand.

"I second-guess everything now. I don't take anything anyone says at face value anymore, and I question everything, evaluating whether I think people are telling the truth or whether I'm being fed a pack of lies." He shakes his head in frustration. "Making decisions on anything, from what I want to have for dinner all the way up to major issues at the company, takes forever because I spend so much time turning over every possible outcome in my head before I can commit. Classic decision paralysis. It's exhausting."

His voice is raw with pain, and I instinctively lean in, pressing my shoulder against his as we stand side by side, staring out at the ocean.

"I'm sorry it's been so hard for you," I say softly. "Hopefully, your confidence will recover with time."

He nods, bending down to snag a small rock off the beach and tossing it gently into the water. "I hope so too."

I crouch down beside him, my fingers sifting through the cool sand until they close around a smooth seashell. Rising, I turn to Jesse, the shell nestled in my palm. Words form on my tongue, but they evaporate the moment our eyes lock.

The air between us crackles with electricity. Jesse's brown eyes, flecked with gold in the fading sunlight, capture mine, and my breath catches in my throat. I want to comfort him, to wrap my arms around him and chase away his doubts. I want to taste those full lips again, to feel the heat of his body against mine.

His eyes flick to my mouth, and for a heartbeat, he seems about to close the distance between us. My pulse races, anticipation coiling in my gut.

Suddenly, a rogue wave surges up the beach, catching us both off guard. Water sloshes around our calves, soaking the hems of our rolled-up jeans.

"Jesus!" he yelps, jumping back.

I let out a startled laugh, the tension of the moment shattered. "Fuck me, that's colder than I thought!"

His rich laughter joins mine, the sound warming me from the inside out. "So much for staying dry," he chuckles, shaking water from his feet.

We share a grin and turn to head back up the beach. As we walk, our hands brush occasionally, sending little sparks up my arm.

Chapter Two

Jesse

Tension crackles between us as Martin and I walk back to the house. The sound of the waves fades behind us, replaced by the soft padding of our feet on the pavement. Neither of us speaks.

I sneak a glance at Martin. Is he regretting that almost-kiss? Or wishing it had turned into more?

Stop. We agreed that night was a one-and-done. We're keeping this professional. Friends.

But the memory of his warmth as he stood so close to me on the beach lingers. The way his eyes flickered to my lips before he darted his tongue out to moisten his own. The way his pupils blew out wide as he stared at me.

I push open the door, and we step inside. The cool air from the AC hits us, a stark contrast to the balmy evening outside.

I can't look at him directly. My gaze darts around the room, settling on anything but his face. The moment plays on repeat in my mind. God, I wanted to kiss him. *I still want to.*

"So, uh…" I start, rubbing the back of my neck. "That was a nice walk." *Oh god. Awkward, much?*

Martin nods, his hands shoved deep in his pockets. "Yeah, it was."

Uncomfortable silence stretches between us. I need to say something, do something to break this tension. But all I can think about is how his lips felt against mine and the way muscles felt under my hands.

Nope. Stop. Not going to happen.

"I, uh… I think I'll turn in early," Martin says, his voice rough. "It's been a busy weekend with the move and all."

"Of course, yeah." I nod, probably too enthusiastically. "Okay, well… Good night."

He hesitates for a moment, then heads for the guest room.

ell

Later that night, I toss and turn in my bed, unable to quiet my mind. I'm acutely conscious of Martin's presence in the house. Every time I close my eyes, I can see the images of that night months ago in my hotel room, only now they're mixed in with the way he looked tonight on the beach. The way the sunlight caught the silvery strands of his hair, his encouraging smile when I confessed how I still struggle after my divorce.

I've been replaying that night in Seattle constantly over the last few months. Up until now, I honestly believed I was misremembering how intense the connection was between us. But now that he's here, in my home, right down the hall, it's pretty clear I wasn't imagining anything. I want him again with a fierceness I don't have words for.

I groan, punching my pillow in frustration. *This is ridiculous. I'm too old for schoolkid crushes and what-ifs.*

It's for the best that nothing happened tonight on the beach. Really. We work together now. It would just complicate everything.

And haven't I had enough complications to last a lifetime?

I roll onto my back, staring at the ceiling. My divorce is still fresh, the wound still raw. I'm not ready for... whatever this is with Martin. *Am I?*

But god, the way he looks at me. Like he sees past all my bullshit, right to my core. Like he understands me.

Stop. You're just lonely. Projecting.

I close my eyes, trying to force myself to sleep, but all I can see is Martin's face. All I can feel is the warmth of his body as he stood next to me on the beach, pressing his shoulder into mine in a small gesture of comfort.

Finally, hours later, I'm beyond frustrated. Sleep seems like a distant dream at this point. I throw off the covers and swing my legs over the side of the bed. Maybe a snack or a drink will help settle my racing mind.

Padding barefoot down the stairs, I make my way to the kitchen. The house is silent, save for the soft hum of the fridge and the distant crash of waves outside. I flick on the light, squinting at the sudden brightness.

Opening the fridge, I scan its contents. Nothing's appealing to me, but I grab a carton of milk anyway. As I reach for a glass from the cupboard, I hear a soft noise behind me.

I turn to find Martin standing beside the kitchen island. He's wearing just a pair of pajama bottoms, his chest bare. My mouth goes dry.

"Couldn't sleep either?" he asks, his voice husky.

I shake my head, trying not to stare. "Nah. Thought maybe some milk might help."

Martin nods, running a hand through his tousled hair. "Mind if I join you?"

"Be my guest," I say, grabbing another glass.

We sit at the island, sipping our milk in silence. The tension from earlier lingers, filling the space between us. I can't help but sneak glances at him, noticing the way the low light plays across his features.

"Jesse," Martin starts, then pauses, as if unsure how to continue.

I look up, meeting his eyes. There's an intensity there that makes my heart race. "Yeah?"

He opens his mouth to speak, then closes it again. The silence stretches between us, charged with unspoken words.

I swallow hard, my throat suddenly as dry as the Sahara. His gaze is intense and I feel exposed under his scrutiny. The kitchen feels too small, too intimate, with just the two of us here in the middle of the night.

"Listen, about earlier..." I start, but he speaks at the same time.

"Jesse, I..." He pauses, taking a deep breath. "I don't want to complicate things."

I nod, relief and disappointment warring inside me. "Right. Of course. We're colleagues. Friends."

"Friends," he echoes, but something in his tone makes my heart skip a beat.

We fall silent again, the only sound the gentle ticking of the clock on the wall. I force my gaze away, staring intently at my glass of milk.

"It's just..." Martin breaks the silence, his voice low. "I can't stop thinking about that night... after *The Open Door* party..."

My head snaps up, eyes wide. "You too?"

A small smile plays at the corners of his mouth. "Yeah, me too."

The admission hangs between us and my heart pounds as I stare into his eyes. Every fiber of my being screams at me to lean in, to close the distance between us, to feel his lips against mine.

But fear paralyzes me. *What if I'm misreading this? What if I mess everything up? There's a lot at stake...* The shelter project, our friendship...

Panic rises in my throat. *I can't do this. I'm not ready.* It's too much, too soon.

Before I can stop myself, I'm on my feet, the barstool scraping loudly against the floor. Martin looks startled, his eyes wide with confusion.

"I, uh... I just remembered," I stammer, clutching my empty milk glass like a lifeline. "I have an early call tomorrow. So, ah, I should probably, um, you know, get some sleep?"

It comes out sounding like a question. *So. Awkward.*

I back away from the island slowly, like I'm trying to escape some kind of wild animal. "Thanks for the company, though! Good night!"

I turn and bolt from the kitchen, hating myself for being such a coward. Once I'm safely inside my room, I lean against the closed door, my heart pounding in my chest. Martin's footsteps fade down the hall followed by the soft click of his bedroom door. The house goes silent again.

I realize I'm still clutching my empty milk glass in my hand. *Smooth, Greenwood.* I roll my eyes and set it down on the nightstand, my fingers shaking slightly. *Fuck, I really am a sad sack.*

I collapse onto my bed, burying my face in my pillow. Sleep seems even more impossible now.

Goddammit. I am well and truly fucked.

Over breakfast the next morning we both act as if whatever happened between us in the kitchen last night was some kind of dream, studiously ignoring it, even though it's constantly on my mind.

Over the next few weeks, we fall into a comfortable rhythm. I usually work from the Greenwood Energy offices three or four days a week, while Martin works from my home office, laying the groundwork for the shelter and job training center I want to build for LGBT young people.

We usually eat dinner together, and then we almost always take a walk on Moonlight Beach.

He's easy to live with, and the truth is, I *love* not coming home to an empty house every night after work.

I noticed after the first few days that he always gets distracted before he can finish his second cup of coffee, inevitably leaving his half-full mug in random places around the house. It's turned into a game between us, with Martin finding ever more ridiculous places to stash his half-empty mug for me to find when I get home. I've discovered it everywhere from the fruit bowl on the kitchen table to tucked inside the mailbox. It makes me laugh every day.

A few days later, I arrive home after a particularly long, hot day spent at a job site in the east part of the county. We're in the middle of a relatively rare heat wave in SoCal, and the temperature this afternoon had soared to over 100 degrees while I was stuck outside helping the contractor solve a thorny solar panel installation issue. Normally the first thing I do when I arrive home is seek out Martin to check in, but right now I'm so uncomfortable, a shower is my top priority.

"Hey, Martin, I'm a disgusting, sweaty mess, so I'm heading straight up to shower," I call, eager to wash off the frustrating afternoon.

After peeling off my clothes, I step under the water with my eyes closed, focusing on how good the cool water feels on my overheated skin. Opening my eyes a moment later, I'm greeted by the sight of his coffee cup, a non-breakable version for today, perched neatly on my soap dish.

My bark of laughter echoes through the bathroom, and somehow it makes my long, hot, miserable afternoon into something funny as opposed to something irritating.

After my shower, I find him in the office.

"You outdid yourself today," I grin, presenting him with the cup.

His warm laugh wraps around my heart, squeezing it in a way I don't want to acknowledge. "Ah, you found it already? I was hoping it'd take you longer."

You know," I say, leaning my hip against his desk, "normal people just finish their coffee."

He swivels in his chair, eyes twinkling with mischief as he beams up at me. "Well, where's the fun in that, Jess?"

I roll my eyes, but I can't keep the smile off my face. It's these silly, funny moments that make me realize how much I've missed laughing. Even before my divorce, life with Andrew hadn't exactly been overflowing with joy, and these few weeks with Martin have showed me what I'd been missing without even realizing it.

"Just wait," Martin says, waggling his eyebrows. "Tomorrow's spot will blow your mind."

"Can't wait," I grin at him, already looking forward to it.

Chapter Three

Martin

Living with Jesse has worked out amazingly well; far better than I could have predicted. We've settled into a routine that's already familiar and comforting. It's an odd combination of domestic bliss and torture.

Every morning I wake to the smell of coffee and the sound of Jesse humming as he putters around in the kitchen. I shuffle downstairs, bleary-eyed, where I find him flipping pancakes or scrambling eggs, all bed head and soft eyes. And every damn morning my heart flips in my chest when I set eyes on him.

He always greets me with a cheerful "Top o' the mornin' to ya," and I snort at his ridiculously bad Irish accent. Then he hands me my coffee, perfectly fixed with the exact right amount of cream and sugar. I look forward to our mornings almost as much as our evening walks on Moonlight Beach.

The days he works from home, we share his small office, and on those days, I'll be damned if I can get anything done. I catch myself staring at the curve of his neck as he bends over his laptop or the way his hands move as he talks animatedly about the shelter plans.

It's maddening, this constant state of want. I'm too old for this shite. But in a strange way, it's also exciting. I feel like a kid with a crush; it's like being young again.

On our evening beach walks, Jesse and I cover every topic under the sun, from politics and history to books and movies. One night, as the sun dipped below the horizon, painting the sky in shades of orange and pink, he surprised me with an out of the blue thought. "You know, I always thought Darth Vader was misunderstood."

I chuckled. "You're a *Star Wars* fan?"

His face lit up. "Are you kidding? I've probably seen each film twenty times at least!"

"Well, fuck me sideways," I laughed. "I thought I was the only middle-aged bloke around here harboring an unhealthy obsession with lightsabers."

We spent the remainder of our walk trading obscure facts and favorite moments from all the movies, our laughter echoing across the beach.

"Have you been to Galaxy's Edge at Disneyland? You know, their *Star Wars* land?" he asked as we were heading back toward the house.

I shook my head.

"Oh, Martin," he sighed dramatically, "you're missing out. It's like stepping right into the movies."

I laughed. "Well, I'll put it on the 'must do while in California' list, then."

He just nodded, a smile playing on his lips.

"Hey, didn't you mention we have an appointment coming up to check out that possible site for the shelter?" he asks a few minutes later.

I nod. "Yeah, with a Realtor. It's an old community center that's been vacant for a while. Could be a good fit, but we'll have to see. It's in a couple of weeks."

"I'm excited to take a look," Jesse says, his enthusiasm infectious. "I mean, this is really happening, isn't it? We're actually going to build this thing."

I smile at his eagerness. It's one of the many things I like about him. His passion, his drive to make a difference.

"We really are," I say with a smile.

The air between us suddenly grows thick with unspoken desire. Our footsteps slow, and I find myself drifting closer to him, drawn by some invisible force. The setting sun paints his face in warm hues, highlighting the flecks of gold in his brown eyes.

His gaze drops to my lips, lingering there. My heart races as the world narrows to just us, the sound of crashing waves fading into the background.

I lean toward him, tilting my head up to catch his eyes. His lips part, his breath warm on my skin.

Suddenly, a burst of shouting and laughter erupts nearby. A group of teenagers races past us, kicking up sand and shattering the moment. We spring apart, startled.

My heart pounds as I try to catch my breath. Jesse runs a hand through his hair, his cheeks flushed. We avoid eye contact, shuffling our feet in the sand.

"I, uh..." Jesse clears his throat. "Should we head back?"

I nod, not trusting my voice.

We walk up the hill in silence. It should probably be awkward, but instead, it's strangely comfortable. The sound of the waves and the chatter of beachgoers fills the air. I sneak a look at him, admiring the way the fading light plays across his features, highlighting the angles of his jaw and the curve of his lips.

And lying in bed that night, I can't stop thinking about him.

Later that week, I'm sitting at my desk in Jesse's home office, enjoying my second cup of coffee. We'd enjoyed our usual banter this morning over a delicious breakfast of eggs and bacon, and a smile plays on my lips as I settle in to figure out what I need to accomplish today. I dig out my old-fashioned planner, which has been buried under a pile of paperwork for the last few days. Yes, I'm that guy. That old relic who can't quite make the full switch to an electronic planner. My breath catches in my throat as I stare, unblinking, at the calendar page of my book. *That can't be right. It's not today... is it?*

Grabbing my cell phone off my desk, I stare at it, unable to believe what I'm seeing. *It's true. It's true and I almost fucking forgot.*

Today is Richard's birthday.

A tidal wave of shame and guilt crashes into me. I shove myself back from the desk, the chair wheels screeching across the hardwood floor.

"Fuck," I mutter, running both hands through my hair. Suddenly, the walls feel like they're closing in, so I stalk out to the living room, bile rising in my throat. My chest constricts with that old, familiar pain as Richard's face flashes through my mind. His mischievous smile. His dark eyes surrounded by laugh lines. His deep, growly voice with the hint of French Canadian accent. The sound of his laughter. The memories hit me so hard and fast I need to sit on the couch and put my head between my knees for a moment.

Never once in almost twenty-five years have I even come close to forgetting this day. It was only a few years ago that I stopped making an annual pilgrimage to Montreal to visit the cemetery where he's buried. I'm always aware of the day's approach for weeks, and it usually looms on the calendar like a specter.

I glance at the clock, quickly calculating the time difference to Montreal. I need to call Celeste. I always talk to Richard's twin sister on this day, but I'm suddenly at a loss for words. Celeste knows me well, and she's incredibly perceptive. *What if she can tell I almost forgot?*

I shake my head because that is ridiculous. She might be able to read me like a book, but the woman's not a bloody psychic.

I reach for my phone, fingers trembling as they hover over her name.

For Christ's sake, I need to cop on and pull myself together.

She answers, her melodic voice warm and familiar. "Martin, mon cher! How are you?"

Her French Canadian accent normally wraps around me like a comforting blanket, but today, it makes my chest ache as jagged shards of guilt stab at me like knives.

"I'm good, Celeste. Happy birthday!"

"Oh, merci, mon ami." She chuckles. "Can you even believe I'm sixty-nine years old today? Mon Dieu, I certainly don't feel it."

"Ah, but you'll be forever young, Celeste." I smile, trying to act normally.

Celeste and I leaned on each other hard through the darkest days of Richard's illness and after his death. I don't think I would have survived everything without her.

"So, tell me about California! How is the new job?"

"It's good. We're making progress on the shelter, and I like San Diego so far."

"And your boss? Jesse, right? What's he like?"

My stomach twists. "He's... dedicated. Hard-working."

I cringe inwardly at my vague responses. This isn't how Celeste and I usually talk. We've always been open with each other, and holding back on her now feels wrong.

As we continue chatting, my mind drifts to Jesse. The way his eyes crinkle when he laughs. How he talks with his hands when he's excited about something.

"Martin?" Her questioning tone jolts me back to the present.

"Sorry, I... What were you saying?"

There's a pause, and I can almost see her brow creased with concern. "Is everything alright? You seem distracted."

"I'm fine," I say, too quickly. "Just... thinking about Richard. You know how it is today."

"Of course," she says softly. "I miss him too. It's difficult to believe he's been gone so many years."

The conversation feels familiar, an annual ritual as we share some of our favorite memories. Normally, this tradition of ours makes me feel good. It brings back some of the best memories of my life, reminding me of how much we loved each other and how lucky I was to find him.

But after we chat a bit longer and end the call, the weight pressing down on my chest grows heavier. I feel raw and exposed. And terrified.

Logically, I know it's absurd to think that having feelings for Jesse is a betrayal of Richard's memory. It's not like I've been celibate since losing him—far from it. But in all these years I've never once been tempted to open my heart to anyone else.

Until now. And it's bloody terrifying.

Chapter Four

Martin

Later that evening, Jesse arrives home from his office and we order dinner before heading out for our beach walk. It's become something of an evening ritual for us, one I've started to look forward to every day. Tonight, though, I'm quiet, lost in my thoughts as we descend the steep, wooden staircase leading down to the beach. We kick off our shoes, and I curl my toes into the sand, my feet instinctively seeking out the last of the sun's warmth that hides underneath that top layer. The crashing waves usually bring me peace, but tonight they seem distant and uninviting. The sky is painted vibrant hues of pink, orange, and purple, but my mind is too jumbled to fully appreciate it.

Jesse looks at me as we make our way slowly along the waterline, his brow furrowed. "Is everything okay? You're awfully quiet tonight."

I hesitate, my throat tight. Part of me wants to brush it off, but Jesse's concerned gaze holds me.

"It's... it's Richard's birthday today," I finally admit, staring out at the ocean but not really seeing it.

"Oh, I'm sorry. This must be a hard day for you." His eyes are full of empathy.

I shrug. "He's been gone a long time, so it's familiar, at least. But some years are harder than others."

He nods before reaching out to grab my hand, giving it a gentle, comforting squeeze.

"Grief isn't a linear process," he says. "I know getting over a divorce isn't the same kind of grief as losing someone you love, but I know about the good days and the bad days."

I shoot him a grateful smile. We continue along for a few more minutes before he says in a quiet voice, "Does it help to talk about him? I'd love to know more about Richard."

I raise my brows in surprise. "You would?"

"Absolutely. Anyone you loved that much must have been special." Jesse smiles, the corners of his eyes crinkling up, reminding me a little of Richard's, and it suddenly occurs to me Jesse is about the same age as Richard was when he died. I don't know what that means, or if it's contributing to my mixed-up feelings around Jesse, but I can't worry about it right now.

I allow myself to relax as memories of my funny, charming, brilliant partner wash over me. "Richard was a force of nature. He was a lawyer. A fierce one. But he was great fun as well. Always knew how to make me laugh, and he made everyone around him comfortable. He was from Montreal, part of a big, tight-knit, French Canadian family." I let out a soft laugh, remembering the fun we used to have on our visits to Quebec. "His twin sister, Celeste, still lives there. I rang her earlier to wish her happy birthday."

"Oh, that's great. How did you two meet?" he asks.

"He was one of the first Americans I ever met—or at least, I thought he was American at the time." I chuckle. "I was twenty, freshly arrived from Ireland. I got the boot when I came out to my family at eighteen, so after a couple of years kicking around Dublin, I took a chance and made my way to America."

Some of the color drains out of Jesse's face, and he swallows hard. "Oh, Martin, I didn't realize your family had kicked you out. I'm so sorry."

I shrug. "It was so long ago it's almost like it happened to someone else. Coming to America was the best decision I ever made."

He nods in response.

"Anyway, I started volunteering at a queer community center right after I got to New York. He volunteered there too, providing pro bono legal advice and services to the community."

It's been a long time since I've allowed myself to play with my memories from those early days in New York. They've taken on an almost antique feeling in my head. Like old photos that have turned yellow with age.

"Oh, right! And there was a movie about you two, right? That's how Penn found you?"

I chuckle. "That sounds a lot more glamorous than it was. But yes, a few years ago, a young, queer filmmaker made a documentary about us. Penn caught it on TV one day, and that's how I ended up at *The Open Door*."

"That's amazing." Jesse shakes his head. "You two did so much good work together."

"I learned so much from him. There was a big age gap between us, almost seventeen years, but we were soul mates in every way I know of."

"How long were you together?"

"I had him almost nine years. We lost him in 1998. He was quite sick for that last year though. By then, we had moved to Philadelphia to start a gay-friendly shelter and community center there."

"Oh, yes, Penn told me that." He pauses for a moment, chewing on his lip before he speaks again. "Do you... Can I ask you a personal question?"

"Of course. Anything," I answer.

"Richard passed away from AIDS, right?"

"I nod. Yes. It was actually an AIDS-related form of pneumonia called PCP."

Jesse nods, still chewing on his lip. "So, can I ask... how did you avoid getting the virus?"

"Well, like I said, Richard had a few years on me. Obviously, we'd both been with other people before we met, but he'd been out there longer. He was a young, gorgeous, relatively wealthy gay man living in Greenwich Village in the '70s and '80s. He was popular and lived his life to the fullest. When we met, because we were both volunteering at the Center, we knew things were risky, and we decided from the start that we were going to always practice safe sex. We were careful from the very beginning."

"Oh, wow. Even though you were exclusive?" he asks.

"We decided to be exclusive pretty quickly after we got together. We figure he probably contracted it sometime in the late 1980s. But he didn't show any symptoms until about 1995. He was officially diagnosed in 1996."

"So the fact that you decided to use condoms all the time..."

"Likely saved my life," I finish for him. "Or at least stopped me from becoming infected."

"Holy shit," he breathes. "Thank god you made that decision."

"Aye. And that was all him. He insisted on it. I would have ditched the condoms a few years after

we were exclusive. We fought about it several times, actually. But it was an issue he would never budge on. He said he would never want to put me at risk." I swallow hard.

"Oh, Martin," Jesse whispers. "I'm so sorry you lost him too soon. He sounds like he was a special person." I turn to look at him, and his eyes are shiny. *God. This man is so sweet. He's so full of goodness and empathy.*

"That he was. Losing him was the worst thing I've ever had to live through, but even knowing what I know now, I wouldn't change anything. My time with him made me who I am."

I pause, unsure if I should say the next thing that comes to mind. *Ah, feck it.* "You know, Jesse... You remind me of him in some ways. You're both eternally optimistic, always looking for the good in people. You have the same ability to find joy in the little things, to be silly and have fun. It's... nice."

It's Jesse's turn to blink at me, and his Adam's apple bobs in his throat as he swallows hard. "Thank you," he whispers, his eyes soft. "I'm glad I can remind you of those happy times."

Friday of the following week, I'm up earlier than normal, since I've a busy day planned. Jesse and I are meeting with a Realtor to check out a possible site for the shelter, but before that I've got several scheduled meetings. I'm not exactly at my best in the mornings, but I manage to make it to the kitchen before Jesse for once. I'm settling into my seat at the breakfast bar clutching my coffee mug like the lifeline it is, when Jesse strolls in, looking far too chipper for this ungodly hour.

"Top o' the morning to ya, Marty," he chirps. I grunt in response, not nearly caffeinated enough for his enthusiasm and his terrible attempt at an Irish accent.

"So," he says, leaning against the counter, a mischievous glint in his eye, "I need you to pack an overnight bag before our meeting with the Realtor today. I'll swing by here to pick you up and we can head out there together."

I blink owlishly at him, not understanding. "Come again?"

"An overnight bag," he repeats, grinning like the cat that got the cream. "You know, clothes, toothbrush, clean undies."

"And why, pray tell, would I need an overnight bag for a meeting with a Realtor?"

Jesse's grin widens. "That's for me to know and you to find out."

I narrow my eyes at him, and he barks out a laugh that makes my heart flip in my chest. *God, he's adorable.*

"Just trust me, okay?" His smile is wicked, and it's stupidly endearing.

I try to tamp down the flutter of anticipation in my stomach. "Fine," I grumble, unsuccessfully trying to sound as if I'm put out.

"Great," he grins. "I know we've both got busy mornings planned, but I'll be back here just after ten to pick you up."

I spend the rest of the morning curious as hell about what he's got planned. It's been years since anyone's surprised me like this, and I'm looking forward to it so much it makes me feel a bit sad. While my lifestyle since losing Richard has certainly been heartache-free, I realize now that it's been missing these little joyful moments. The kind you can only experience when you let someone get close. But before I go too far down that particular rabbit hole, I force myself to focus on gathering what I'll need for tonight.

A few hours later, come back downstairs, bag in hand, to find Jesse waiting by the door, practically bouncing on his toes. "Ready?" he asks, eyes sparkling.

"As I'll ever be," I reply, unable to keep the smile off my face. "Lead on, mystery man."

An hour later, we pull up to a dilapidated building that's seen better days. Graffiti covers the walls, and weeds poke through cracks in the concrete. But there's potential here. I can see it.

As we step out of the car, a young man approaches us with a million-dollar smile. "Mr. Greenwood? Mr. Benoit? I'm Cassidy, your Realtor."

Christ on a bike. Cassidy looks like he stepped out of a fashion magazine—tall and lithe, with sun-kissed skin and perfectly tousled blond hair. His crisp white shirt and tailored slacks hug his body in all the right places, and his bright blue eyes sparkle with charm. He's exactly my type. Normally, I'd be eyeing him for a night of fun. No strings, no complications, just pure physical pleasure. But strangely, there's not even a flicker of interest from below my belt.

He extends his hand, and I shake it with a friendly smile. "Nice to meet you, Cassidy."

"The pleasure's all mine," he purrs, his eyes roaming over me in a way that leaves little doubt about his interest.

I clear my throat, acutely aware of Jesse standing beside me. "So, shall we take a look?"

"Of course," Cassidy says, flashing us another mega-watt smile. "Right this way, gentlemen."

As Cassidy leads us through the building, I can't help but notice the way he moves, all fluid grace and subtle invitation. Normally, a guy like this would have my full attention. I'd be plotting how to get him alone, maybe suggest grabbing a drink after the tour. But today? Nothing. Nada. Not even a whisper of interest.

Instead, my eyes keep drifting to Jesse. He's examining the space with intense focus, that adorable little crease forming between his brows as he considers the potential of this run-down building. When he turns to Cassidy with a question about the property's zoning, I'm struck by the warmth in his soulful brown eyes.

As we continue the tour, Cassidy's flirting shifts into overdrive. He constantly touching me—a hand on my arm as he points out a feature, fingers brushing mine as he hands over some paperwork. It's blatant and unmistakable, but to my surprise, my body isn't responding at all. No quickening pulse, no flush of heat. Nothing.

I sneak a glance at Jesse, who seems uncharacteristically quiet. His jaw is set, and there's a tightness around his eyes that wasn't there before. *Is he... jealous?*

Before I can ponder that question further, Jesse's phone rings. He frowns at the screen. "Sorry, I need to take this. It's the office." He steps away, leaving me alone with the attractive, young Realtor.

The moment Jesse's out of earshot, Cassidy's flirting hits a new high. He steps closer, invading my personal space. "So, Martin," he purrs, his voice low and sultry. "I would love to take you for a drink sometime. I live in Hillcrest, and there's an amazing new place right in my neighborhood that just opened up, that I'm dying to try."

His hand trails down my arm as he licks his lips suggestively.

I'm about to firmly shut him down when I hear footsteps approaching. Jesse rounds the corner, his expression darkening when he sees us.

Chapter Five

Jesse

I freeze in my tracks, the sight before me sending a surge of heat through my body, and not the good kind. Cassidy, that slick, pretty-boy, is leaning in way too close to Martin, his hand resting on Martin's forearm. Martin's polite smile doesn't reach his eyes, but Cassidy doesn't seem to notice or care, and his intentions are crystal fucking clear.

"So, there's this new place—"

I clear my throat loudly, interrupting him and purposely inserting myself between them as Martin takes a step back from the younger man.

Slimy little prick. He looks like one of those smarmy asswipes from some stupid real-estate reality show, *Gazillion Dollar Listing* or whatever the fuck. His overly coiffed hair and his perfectly capped, white teeth ooze counterfeit confidence, making my skin crawl. He's eyeing Martin like he's some kind of prize, and my jaw ticks audibly as I grit my teeth. *If he thinks he's going to have Martin for dinner, he's got another think coming.*

Cassidy straightens, shifting his gaze to me, letting his eyes drag over my body. He darts his tongue out to moisten his lips, and I have to conceal a visible shudder. *Ick.*

"I was just getting to know Martin here a bit better. We were discussing dinner plans. Maybe you'd *both* be interested in... dinner." His tone is suggestive, making me want to throttle him.

Not fucking likely.

"No, I don't think that will work." I can't keep the edge out of my voice. *Who does this little fucker think he is?* And seriously, talk about unprofessional. "Actually, I don't think this building is quite what we're looking for. It doesn't have the right feel for our project," I say, crossing my arms and staring him down like I'm some kind of gunslinger, daring him to make another move.

This behavior isn't like me. Normally, I'm the king of avoiding confrontation at almost all costs, but something about seeing this guy hit on Martin right in front of me makes my blood boil.

Martin looks at me, a flicker of amusement in his eyes.

Cassidy blinks, his demeanor changing abruptly. *Yeah, you little son of a bitch. You see how it is now? Keep it in your pants, motherfucker.*

"Oh, of course, of course," he stammers, glancing between Martin and me, suddenly unsure of himself. "Well, we can always keep looking. I'm sure we can find something to suit your needs."

"Thanks for your time," Martin says amicably. "We'll be in touch if we have any questions."

"Of course," he repeats.

We make our way quickly to the exit, and I watch like a hawk as he extends his hand to Martin. A low, possessive growl escapes my throat when the handshake lasts a half second too long, and I catch Martin's eye. He looks like he's trying to hold back a laugh, his green eyes twinkling.

Cassidy doesn't even bother extending a hand to me, which is probably best for his safety since I'm liable to tear his entire arm off. Instead, he gives me a watery smile and directs a halfhearted wave in my general direction before hightailing it in the direction of his white BMW like his ass is on fire.

We walk back to my car in silence, the sun beating down on us, tension thick in the air. My mind races, trying to make sense of my own behavior. *Where the hell did that come from?* I've never reacted like that before with anyone, not even Andrew.

A knot forms in my stomach as my ex's face flashes through my mind. *All those years and I never knew. Never suspected.* For the billionth time, I ask myself how I could have possibly been so blind. Anger and shame wash over me as I slide behind the wheel of my car. *Has Andrew's betrayal turned me into some kind of possessive, jealous asshole?* The thought makes me sick.

But mixed in with all the confusion is an unfamiliar feeling. I think I feel... powerful... Strong... I survived that confrontation, even though I hate shit like that. But I wasn't about to lie down and let myself, or someone I care for, get taken advantage of. I didn't want that guy flirting with Martin, but at the same time, it looked like Martin wasn't into it. So maybe it wasn't all jealousy. Maybe it was... protective. I don't want Martin to get hurt. Don't want him falling for some smooth-talking pretty boy who'd just use him and toss him aside. But what if I read the situation all wrong? What if Martin was interested in Cassidy and I just cockblocked him? That would make me nothing more than a jealous asshole.

"Jesse," Martin says, placing a gentle hand on my forearm. "You alright? You seem a tad off." I realize we're sitting here roasting in the hot car as I'm staring into space, my mind spinning with these unwelcome thoughts.

"Oh, no, I'm fine," I say, clearing my throat, pressing the car's Start button and cranking up the air-conditioning.

"So, um... what did you think?" I ask, not sure if I'm asking what he thought about the building or about whatever just happened with Cassidy.

"The location has potential, but we should see a few other sites before making a decision," he says. "We have time."

"Right." I tap my fingers on the steering wheel, searching for something else to say. The words tumble out of my mouth before I can stop them. "Listen, Martin, about Cassidy... He, um, seemed pretty interested in you. I, ah... I hope I didn't screw that up for you. I mean, I don't want you to feel awkward or anything, just because we're working together or roommates or whatever..." I clear my throat awkwardly. "But, um, I kind of got the impression up there that maybe you weren't into him, and uh..." My voice trails off awkwardly.

I wait, my heart pounding as Martin stays silent. *Shit. I've totally misread everything. He's pissed off.* I grip the steering wheel tightly, bracing myself for his anger.

Finally, Martin speaks. "Jesse, you didn't screw anything up." His voice is soft, reassuring. The tension in my shoulders eases a bit. "I wasn't interested in Cassidy at all. To be honest, I found his flirting a bit... uncomfortable."

I let out a breath I didn't realize I was holding. "Oh, okay. Okay. Good."

He nods, a small smile playing on his lips. "Really. I appreciate you looking out for me. It means a lot."

Relief washes over me, but it's quickly followed by a surge of something else. Something hot and exciting that I'm not quite ready to name. I've never seen myself in the role of a protector before. But I think maybe I like it.

I suck in a breath, the cool air from the air-conditioning filling my lungs. "Okay. Good." I take a deep breath. I guess now is the time to tell him about my plans for the weekend. *Shit, I hope he likes the idea.*

"Okay, then," I say again. "I, uh, I actually have a surprise for you."

Martin turns toward me with a quizzical look. "Oh? What would that be?"

I take a deep breath. "Well, I know Richard's birthday was a tough day for you, so I thought you could use a bit of a break." I swallow before continuing, nervous as hell, for some reason. "Anyway, I thought, maybe, you might like to go to Disneyland and check out Galaxy's Edge. So I made us some reservations for this weekend at the Grand Californian Hotel and got us park tickets."

For a second, his expression is unreadable while he stares at me in silence.

Panic flares in my chest. *Shit, did I go too far? Have I somehow fucked everything up by planning something so... relationshippy? Fuck. Fuck. Fuck.*

But suddenly, the car fills with the sound of his laughter, and relief floods through me. "You're serious? We're going to Disneyland?" His eyes sparkle with childlike excitement.

I grin, nodding. "Yeah. All we've really done since you arrived is work. I want to show you California, and what better place to start than the happiest place on Earth, right?"

Martin reaches over and squeezes my arm, his touch sending shivers down my spine. "Jesse, this is brilliant. No one has surprised me like this in... forever. Thank you. Truly, thank you so much."

I glance at him, ready to bask in his excitement, but I'm shocked when I realize his eyes are glassy with unshed tears. I've never seen him vulnerable like this, not even on Richard's birthday.

My heart clenches, and I'm overwhelmed with the desire to touch him. I want to brush my thumb across his cheek and catch those tears before they fall. To pull him close and breathe him in. My fingers twitch on the steering wheel, itching to feel his skin under them.

I drop my eyes to his lips, and I'm hit with a vivid memory of how they felt against mine that night in Seattle. Soft, warm, eager. He tasted of whiskey and lust and something uniquely Martin. My mouth goes dry, and I have to swallow hard.

The air in the car is thick, and every cell in my body is screaming at me to lean over and kiss him. I'm dying to see if the intensity of that night in Seattle was real or if it was just some alcohol-fueled fantasy that I've been nurturing for all these months.

Now, though, there's more than just physical attraction between us. There's something about Martin that makes my feelings run deeper, making me want more than just sex. His wit, his compassion, the way he listens like every word I say matters. I want to peel back all his layers, to know every secret, every fear, every dream. I want to know all about his past, and

I desperately want to be part of his present. And, maybe, part of his future.

I force myself to look away, gripping the steering wheel so tightly, my knuckles go white. My heart beats so loudly he can probably hear it banging into my ribcage.

It wouldn't work. It would be silly to try it. We decided to leave things as friends, and that's fine. It's fine. We're working together. It wouldn't be professional. The list of reasons I shouldn't lean in and kiss him runs on a loop through my head.

The problem is none of the reasons currently running through my mind seem to be anywhere near as powerful as my desire to feel him pressed up against me again.

Chapter Six

Martin

The air in the car crackles with tension. I can see the hunger and lust swirling in Jesse's eyes. His gaze flickers to my lips, and for a moment, I think he's going to close the distance between us. My heart races, anticipation building in my chest. But then, as quickly as it appeared, the moment shatters. He breaks eye contact, clearing his throat and shifting in his seat.

Disappointment lances through me. *God, I want him to kiss me.* I want him to use me, to take what he needs. I want to be the one to give him everything he craves, just like I did that one night in Seattle. A shiver runs through me just thinking about it.

"So, let's be on our way," he says, shifting the car into drive. "Traffic will be heavy getting up to Anaheim since it's Friday, but we can check in to the hotel and then decide if we want to go into the park tonight."

"That sounds perfect," I say.

We chat comfortably on the drive, but the moments of silence are just as nice. I take in the stunning views as we head north on Interstate 5. The beach communities of Orange County are spectacular, with large mansions perched on the hills rising above the bright blue Pacific Ocean. It feels like we're driving into a postcard.

I'm surprised at how turned on I was by Jesse's apparent jealousy over Cassidy's flirting. Watching this sweet, gentle man go full caveman on the unsuspecting man lit a fire inside me. The way his eyes darkened, his jaw clenched tight, as he stepped between me and Cassidy... It was primal, possessive, and incredibly fucking hot.

I've never had someone react that way over me before. Like he couldn't stand the thought of another man even looking at me, let alone flirting with me. The intensity of his reaction sends a thrill down my

spine, awakening some part of me I never knew exist-
ed.

I shift in my seat, trying to ignore the growing heat
in my groin. He cares about me—I mean if he was
willing to fight for me, that's a logical assumption,
right?

But it's not just that. The message that he wants
me for himself—only for himself—is doing strange
things to me. *I like it. A lot.* More than I probably
should, considering our working relationship and the
fact that we're living under the same roof. But God,
the hunger in his eyes when he looks at me damn near
brings me to my knees sometimes.

I sneak a glance at him as he drives, his strong hands
gripping the steering wheel. I want to reach out and
touch him, to feel the warmth of his skin under my
fingertips.

But I don't.

Intricate stonework and timber adorn the façade of
the hotel we pull up to a few hours later. I still can't

believe Jesse booked this trip for us. For me. I'd mentioned my love of *Star Wars* almost in passing. It's such a small thing. But he noticed and then used the info to do something special for me. It's been so long since I've felt these kinds of warm, fuzzy feelings I don't know what to do with them.

But that's future Martin's problem. Right now it's time to focus on having some fun because it's been too long for that too.

Jesse flashes me a mischievous grin as he passes his keys to the valet. "We get our own entry gate and an extra hour of early access to the park from this hotel."

"I've never met a grown man so excited about Disneyland." I'm teasing, but I find his enthusiasm incredibly endearing. More than endearing, really.

He chuckles and waggles his eyebrows at me in response. On our way to the front desk, we pass a collection of plush couches gathered around a huge stone fireplace. They're occupied by several sets of exhausted-looking parents enjoying a drink or a snack while keeping an eye on little ones roaming around.

After checking in, we head to our luxury two-bedroom suite. Emphasis on *luxury*. Lush living and dining areas, two bedrooms, each with a king bed. I'm not unaccustomed to the finer side of life—Richard and his family had more money than they knew what to do with,—but this feels more like living out a childhood dream than two friends getting away for a weekend. I let out a laugh as I check out the room, delighted. "You're really spoiling me," I say with a grin. "Keep this up and you'll never be rid of me."

He beams at me. "You'll hear no complaints about that from me."

My heart flutters in my chest, and I fight to shove the feelings aside. But then he lets his gaze roam over me, sending a hot shiver through my body. A rush of blood surges directly to my cock as images of that night in his Seattle hotel room flood my mind.

Maybe hotels bring out a different side of Jesse? Whatever the reason is, I very much like hotel-Jesse.

"How about we save the park for tomorrow?" he suggests, pulling me out of my daydream as he glances out the window. "I don't know about you, but I'd like to wash the Friday traffic off me. We could go into Downtown Disney for dinner and to watch the fireworks from the hotel's special lounge."

"Sounds like a top-notch idea," I reply before wandering over to the inviting-looking sectional in front of the gas fireplace, flopping onto it with a sigh. "I'll be getting on that right away. I promise."

I don't know whether it's the hotel itself, the comfortable suite, or the subtle change in Jesse's demeanor since the incident with Cassidy, but I feel more relaxed right now than I have in recent memory.

Jesse chuckles and disappears into his room to shower while I allow my eyes to drift shut. I just need a couple of minutes to relax before making myself presentable for public consumption.

A while later, a gentle hand on my chest pulls me from the depths of sleep. I blink my eyes open to find Jesse sitting on the edge of the couch next to me, a playful grin on his lips.

"Falling asleep already? We just got here," he teases. His hand lingers on my chest, the pressure causing a delicious heat to spread through my torso down to my belly.

He traces circles with his fingertips on my shirt as we hold each other's gaze. It's as if time has been suspended, like we're the only two people in existence.

His tongue sneaks out to wet his lips, and my cock jumps.

"So," he murmurs, the single word coming out low and growly. The heat in my abdomen spreads lower. "Dinner..."

His touch is driving me half-mad, even through the fabric of my shirt. It's intimate and familiar, and full of anticipation. He has to be able to feel the crazy way my heart is pounding against my rib cage.

His hand remains on my chest, his eyes holding mine captive as he leans closer. I know what he wants. And he's about to get it.

"Fuck dinner," I mutter under my breath, and before I can talk myself out of it, I reach up with one hand, curling it around the back of his neck and pulling him down at the same time as I rise up to capture his mouth with mine.

He moans, the hand on my chest tightening into a fist, gripping my shirt like he's afraid I might disappear.

Every nerve ending in my body sparks to life as his tongue traces the seam of my lips, and I part them eagerly, inviting him inside.

I slide my fingers into his hair, tugging lightly, and he groans into my mouth. The sound shoots straight to my cock, making it throb against the confines of my jeans.

He releases his death grip on my shirt, sliding his hand down my chest to my abdomen, coming to rest on my hip. His thumb sneaks under the hem, brushing against my bare skin, and I shudder.

It's too much and not enough all at once. I'm drowning in sensation, in the scent of his cologne, the wet slide of his lips and tongue, the heat of his body pressing me into the cushions. I never want it to end.

I keep his mouth pressed to mine while nudging him gently so he's stretched out on top of me. His taller frame blankets me, blocking out all other sensory input. Our bodies fit together perfectly, and he's the only thing I can feel. He moans, sending another rush of heat through my veins.

I spread my legs, and he settles between them, his hard length pressing relentlessly against mine. I can't hold back a tortured groan as he grinds into me. Jesus fuck, he feels incredible.

I should really stop this.

The last time we were together, we didn't have a professional relationship to worry about, but things are different now; I mean, technically speaking, he's my employer. This kind of thing rarely leads to anything good.

But I cannot be arsed to care right now. Not with the way he's sucking on my tongue, nearly consuming me and groaning like a starving man enjoying a five-star meal.

God almighty. I haven't wanted anyone this badly in so long. It's almost refreshing to feel the ache in my balls, that *craving* for another person. My hookup-heavy lifestyle is satisfying enough, but this kind of desperation to be close... this desire for *connection*. This is something I haven't felt since Richard.

That gives me pause, but just for a moment. I don't want to examine it too closely. All I want right now is to revel in these amazing feelings.

Jesse's tongue traces a scorching path down my neck, making my heart pound and my head swim. His touch is electric. Last time, we fucked like we were starving for it. But this... this is slow and languid and seems to tap into something deeper. It sparks a need I didn't even know I had.

He slips his hand under my shirt, his palm warm on my skin, causing goose bumps to break out across my flesh. I arch into him, silently urging him on. His mouth finds the pulse point at my collarbone, and he sucks, hard. I gasp. It's like he's branding me, marking me as his own. *Why is that so sexy?*

Heat curls in my belly, tightening and spreading outward like flames, scorching me from the inside out. I feel like he's setting my soul on fire with lust. All I can think is *more, more, more...* and I need it *now.*

He moves, sliding off the couch onto his knees, and urges me to sit up. My pulse thunders in my ears as he kneels between my parted thighs, his heated look making my mouth go dry.

He reaches for my belt as I suck in a sharp breath. With deft fingers, he undoes the buckle and pulls it free from the loops, letting it clatter to the floor. The button and zipper follow, and I lean back, lifting my hips to allow him to tug my clothes down my thighs and all the way off.

My achingly hard cock springs free. He licks his lips, his eyes roaming hungrily over my length. The tip is already slick with precome, glistening in the dim light. I can't tear my eyes away from the sight of him settling between my splayed thighs.

Anticipation coils tightly in my gut as he leans in, ghosting his breath over my sensitive skin. I bite back a whimper as he wraps one hand around the base and leans in, his breath hot against my aching flesh. I suck in a sharp breath, fighting the urge to buck my hips and chase that delicious heat.

His tongue darts out, tracing a hot, wet path along the underside of my shaft. A guttural groan escapes my lips as he swirls it around the swollen head. I tangle my fingers in his hair, scraping my nails lightly against his scalp, needing to hold onto him to ground myself.

"Fuck, Jesse..." I rasp, my voice thick with need.

He hums in response, and the vibrations send delicious tremors through my cock. Then he sinks down, taking me deeper into the wet heat of his mouth. I throw my head back, squeezing my eyes shut as wave after wave of molten pleasure courses through me.

He hollows his cheeks as he sucks me hard, his tongue working skilled magic along my length. He bobs his head, taking me deeper with each downward slide until my cock nudges the back of his throat. He hums again, and looks up at me, his eyes full of heat and need.

My hips flex of their own accord, fucking shallowly into that divine heat. He groans around me like he's savoring the taste and feel of my length filling his mouth.

"Shit, I'm not going to last..." I pant, my fingers tightening in his hair.

Our eyes lock. It's obscenely sexy, the way his lips are stretched around me, his eyes glassy and his cheeks flushed red. Anticipation coils in my groin. My thighs tremble, my toes curling against the carpet as that tight, tingling heat builds. Jesse doubles down on his efforts, his tongue swirling wickedly.

I'm right on the razor's edge, every nerve ending firing as that knot of ecstasy pulls tighter and tighter.

With a hoarse shout, I let go, arching up off the couch as I spill down Jesse's throat in hot pulses. He swallows it all greedily, milking me for every last drop until I collapse back against the cushions in a boneless heap.

He pulls back, a smug, satisfied grin on his face. He licks his lips slowly as our eyes meet. Christ, seeing him so thoroughly debauched, his lips swollen and slick, his eyes still bright with lust has my spent cock giving a valiant twitch.

Chapter Seven

Jesse

I kneel on the floor in front of Martin, feeling pretty damn pleased with myself, because he looks completely blissed out. His eyes dark with lust and slightly unfocused, while his breathing fast and shallow. I love that I can affect him like this.

Unfortunately, however, my 44-year-old knees are complaining, so I reluctantly get to my feet, extending my hand to him.

He looks at me with hooded eyes, his gaze traveling down my body, coming to rest on my cock, which is still obviously hard in my shorts.

He licks his lips, reaching for me. "Mmm. My turn now," he says.

I step out of his reach with a teasing smile on my face.

"Nope, come with me to the bedroom. I don't know about you, but my knees are too old for this kind of fun on a hard floor. We're taking this to the bed. I refuse to rush this."

His eyes flash with desire as he stands, taking a moment to discard his shirt before following me into the bedroom I claimed earlier.

We stand in front of each other for a few moments. It's almost unbearably sexy to stand there fully dressed while Martin is completely naked.

As hot as it is, though, I'm more interested in getting naked so I can feel his skin against mine, so I reach back between my shoulders to pull my shirt over my head.

He licks his lips as he takes me in, and then steps forward, running his hands over my pecs. My eyes flutter shut. Feeling his hands on me is like heaven.

Wordlessly, he undoes my shorts and they fall to the floor around my feet. I step out of them without breaking eye contact. He steps into my space, but to my dismay, avoids my aching, straining cock. Instead, he turns us before pushing me gently backward until my calves hit the bed. I sit on the edge, but he keeps pushing at my shoulders.

"Scoot back to the pillows," he directs. "I want you to be comfortable. Because I plan on taking my time. Did you bring supplies?"

"In the bedside drawer," I groan, and slide back so my head is on the pillows, and he wastes no time climbing onto the bed and straddling me, his knees on either side of my hips.

He plants his mouth on mine and lets out a sexy as fuck groan. "Oh, god, I can taste myself on you," he whispers hoarsely.

Fuck, that's hot. I moan into his mouth as his tongue probes deeper.

I grab his hips, pulling him down, his cock sliding against mine, and we both moan at the delicious friction. He breaks the kiss to trail his mouth down my neck, sucking a mark into the sensitive skin just below my ear.

"You taste so good," he murmurs, his warm breath sending shivers down my spine. "Can't get enough of you."

He rocks his hips again, dragging the length of his cock against mine, and I dig my fingers into the firm globes of his ass to pull him closer. He lets out a breathy chuckle against my collarbone.

"Easy, love. We've got all night, remember? Let me take care of you properly."

With that, he shifts lower, placing hot open-mouthed kisses down my chest and abdomen. My cock twitches and strains toward him as he settles between my spread thighs, those gorgeous green eyes locked on mine as he licks a wet stripe up the underside of my shaft.

The way he's looking at me, like I'm the most delicious thing he's ever seen, is so intense it's almost a physical sensation. His tongue swirls around the head of my cock and I let out a low groan, fisting my hands in the sheets.

He takes me deeper into his mouth and I have to squeeze my eyes shut at the incredible wet heat surrounding me. He bobs his head, his cheeks hollowed, and I feel the pressure building already. "Fuck, Martin...gonna come too fast if you keep that up," I rasp out in warning.

He pulls off with a wicked grin, giving me a chance to catch my breath. "Easy there. Told you I plan on taking my time." He licks a long stripe up the underside of my shaft and I shudder. "Want you nice and relaxed for what I have in mind next."

I groan, my hips bucking involuntarily as he continues his exquisite torture. His tongue traces patterns along my cock, teasing and tantalizing. I'm torn between wanting to let go and the orgasm to overtake me, and holding back, trying to savor every second of this pleasure.

"Martin," I gasp, threading my fingers through his hair. "You're driving me crazy."

He looks up at me, a mischievous glint in his eyes. "That's the idea, love."

Without warning, he takes me deep into the back of his throat, and I cry out, overwhelmed by the sensation. My toes curl as he works me with his mouth, alternating between long, slow strokes and quick, intense suction.

I'm teetering on the edge, my breath coming in short pants. "Fuck, I'm close... I'm gonna-"

He pulls off suddenly, leaving me aching and desperate. I whimper at the loss of contact, but he just grins, crawling back up my body.

"Not yet," Martin whispers with a wicked smile.

My whole body thrums with need, every nerve ending on fire. I groan in frustration, my hips lifting off the bed, seeking friction.

"Oh, god, please," I pant, not caring how desperate I sound.

He chuckles, a low, sexy sound that sends shivers down my spine. "Patience, love. I'm not done with you yet."

His hands roam over my chest, teasing my nipples into hard peaks. I arch into his touch, craving more. He leans down, capturing my lips in a searing kiss and leaving me breathless again.

"Turn over," he murmurs against my mouth.

I comply eagerly, rolling onto my stomach. Martin's hands smooth down my back, kneading the muscles. I moan into the pillow as his thumbs dig into a particularly tight spot near my shoulder blades.

"God, you're gorgeous," he breathes, pressing a kiss to the nape of my neck.

His lips trail down my spine, leaving goosebumps in their wake. I shiver as he reaches the small of my back, his beard tickling my sensitive skin.

"Lift your hips," Martin instructs, his voice husky with desire.

I obey, pushing up onto my knees. He grips my ass, spreading me open. I tense in anticipation, my breath catching in my throat.

The first swipe of his tongue against my hole makes me cry out, burying my face in the pillow to muffle the sound. He hums in approval, the vibration sending jolts of pleasure through me.

"That's it," he murmurs. "Let me hear you."

He dives back in, licking and sucking with enthusiasm. I'm a writhing mess beneath him, pushing back against his face, desperate for more. My neglected cock throbs between my legs.

"Martin," I gasp, "Please, I need-"

He pulls back, leaving me aching and empty. "What do you need, Jesse?" he asks, his voice rough. "Tell me."

I turn my head, meeting his intense gaze over my shoulder. "You," I breathe. "I need you inside me. Please."

"Mmm. And I will be," he says. "But not until I'm good and ready," his eyes twinkle with lust and delight, and I groan in frustration, my excitement ratcheting impossibly higher.

I'm trembling with need, my whole body aching for his touch. His words send a shiver down my spine, and I push my hips back, silently begging for more.

"Please," I whimper, beyond caring how desperate I sound. "I need you so bad."

He chuckles, a low, sexy sound that makes my cock twitch. "Patience, love. I want to savor every inch of you."

His hands knead my ass, spreading me open again. His breath is hot against my sensitive skin just before his tongue darts out, circling my hole. I cry out, burying my face in the pillow to muffle the sound.

"None of that," Martin says, giving my ass a playful smack. "I told you, I want to hear you. Let it out. Let me hear what I do to you."

He dives back in, his tongue working me open with slow, deliberate strokes. I moan shamelessly, pushing back against his face, desperate for more. My neglected cock throbs between my legs, leaking pre-cum onto the sheets.

"God, Martin, fuck yes. You. Oh, fuck yes." I'm a babbling mess, with no chance of a coherent sentence slipping out. I'm nothing but a bag of sensations.

He hums in response, the vibration sending jolts of pleasure through me. I feel like I'm on fire, every nerve ending alive and sparking with sensation. His beard scratches deliciously against my skin as he works, adding another layer of stimulation that threatens to push me over the edge.

Just when I think I can't take anymore, Martin pulls back. I whine at the loss, feeling empty and desperate.

"Shh," he soothes, running his hands down my back. "I've got you, love."

I hear the snap of a bottle cap, and then his slick finger is circling my entrance. He pushes in slowly, and I bear down, welcoming the intrusion.

"That's it," Martin murmurs, working his finger in and out. "You're so tight. So perfect."

He adds a second finger, stretching me carefully. The burn is exquisite, a perfect blend of pleasure and pain that has me writhing on the sheets. He crooks his fingers, searching, and when he finds my prostate, I see stars.

"Oh fuck!" I cry out, my back arching. "Right there. Please, don't stop. God don't stop."

I'm lost in a haze of pleasure as he works me open. I'm dimly aware that I'm babbling, a stream of incoherent pleas and praises falling from my lips.

"Please," I gasp, desperately pleading and wantonly rocking my ass against his fingers inside me. "I'm ready. I need you inside me."

He leans over me, his chest pressing against my back. His lips brush my ear as he whispers, "Are you sure, love? I don't want to hurt you."

I turn my head, catching his gaze. The intensity in his eyes takes my breath away. "I'm sure," I pant. "Please. Put your cock inside me. I can't wait."

He nods, pressing a quick kiss to my shoulder before pulling back. I hear the crinkle of a condom wrapper, then the slick sound of Martin lubing himself up. My heart races in anticipation.

Martin positions himself behind me, the blunt head of his cock pressing against my entrance. He pushes in slowly, giving me time to adjust. The stretch burns in the most delicious way, and I moan, long and low.

"Oh, fuck," Martin groans as he bottoms out. "You're strangling my cock. God, you're so tight. So perfect."

He stills as he bottoms out, letting me get used to the feeling of fullness. I'm trembling, overwhelmed by the sensation and the emotion of having him inside me. After a moment, I rock my hips, silently asking for more.

Martin takes the hint, pulling out almost all the way before thrusting back in. He sets a steady rhythm, each stroke sending sparks of pleasure through my body. I push back to meet him, wanting him deeper, harder.

"Yes," I moan. "God, just like that. Don't stop."

He grips my hips, pulling me back onto his cock with each thrust. The sound of our skin slapping together fills the room, mixed with our gasps and moans. It's raw and primal and absolutely perfect.

I'm lost in a haze of pleasure, every nerve ending on fire as Martin drives into me. His cock hits my prostate with each thrust, sending shockwaves of ecstasy through my body. I'm moaning shamelessly, but I can't bring myself to care.

"Fuck, Martin," I gasp, pushing back to meet his thrusts. "So good... "

He leans over me, blanketing my body with his, his chest pressed against my back. The change in angle has me seeing stars, and I cry out, fisting my hands in the sheets.

"That's it, love," Martin murmurs in my ear, his voice rough with exertion and arousal. "Let me hear you. You sound so beautiful."

His words send a shiver down my spine, and I turn my head, seeking his lips. We kiss messily, all tongue and teeth, as he continues to fuck into me.

I can feel the pressure building in my core, my neglected cock throbbing between my legs. "Martin," I pant against his mouth. "I'm close... so close..."

He snakes a hand around my waist, wrapping his fingers around my aching shaft. "Come for me," he growls. "Want to feel you come apart around me."

It only takes a few strokes of his hand before I'm tumbling over the edge. I cry out Martin's name as my orgasm crashes over me, my vision whiting out as waves of pleasure course through my body. I clench around his cock, and he groans, his hips stuttering as he follows me over the edge.

We collapse onto the bed, a tangle of sweaty limbs and heaving chests. Martin carefully pulls out, and I whimper at the loss. He disposes of the condom and then gathers me into his arms, pressing a soft kiss to my temple.

Chapter Eight

Martin

I lie sprawled across Jesse's chest, our bodies still tangled together, a thin sheen of sweat cooling on our skin. My fingers trace lazy patterns through the light dusting of hair on his chest, and the steady thump of his heartbeat beneath my palm is comforting.

"That was..." I trail off, unable to find the right words.

He chuckles, the sound rumbling through his chest. "Yeah, it was."

I tilt my head up to look at him, drinking in the sight of his flushed cheeks and tousled hair. His eyes are closed, a contented smile playing on his lips. He looks utterly relaxed.

"You're gorgeous like this," I murmur before I can stop myself.

His eyes flutter open, and he gazes at me with such warmth it makes my breath catch. "Look who's talking," he says, running his fingers through my hair.

I hum contentedly, nuzzling into his touch. We fall into a comfortable silence, just basking in each other's presence. It's been so long since I've felt this... peaceful. This connected to another person.

Suddenly, the silence is broken when my stomach lets out an embarrassingly loud growl. Jesse's body shakes with laughter beneath me.

"Hungry?" he teases, poking my side playfully.

I arch an eyebrow at him. "I'm a growing boy, you know. And, if you recall, we missed dinner."

"Mmm." He smiles. "Should I apologize for distracting you?"

I snort a laugh. "I suppose I'll let it go this time. But if you don't get some food into me right quick, I'm going to have to eat you." I lean up and suck his earlobe into my mouth, tickling it with my tongue before biting down on it playfully.

"Eep!" He jumps, letting out a most unmanly but totally adorable squeak. "Let's get some food in you before you start gnawing on the furniture or resorting to cannibalism."

Jesse orders room service, and soon, we're arranged on the bed with a smorgasbord of delicious finger foods spread out in front of us like a picnic.

We eat in comfortable silence for a while, occasionally stealing bites from each other's plates. It's domestic in a way that should probably scare me, but instead, it just feels... right.

"Seeing as you grew up in California, I imagine you're as familiar with Disneyland as you are with the back of your hand, eh?" I tease as we laze on the bed, chatting about our plans for the next day in the park.

Jesse laughs. "I've spent my fair share of time here, I'll admit. But since my nieces and nephews have grown up, I haven't come nearly as often as I used to," he says with a slightly wistful look in his eye. "We used to love bringing them here. It really is a magical place for kids," he says.

"Did you and your ex used to bring them? Give their mum and dad a nice break?" I ask, but Jesse snorts.

"Oh, god, no, Andrew was not a fan of Disneyland. I used to come along when Jeff and Dani would take them, and then when they got older, I would bring them on my own. Actually—" He pauses. "—Andrew wasn't a fan of kids in general." He scoffs. "Which is why it's so very ironic what happened."

I raise an eyebrow. "What do you mean?"

He grabs his wine glass from the nightstand and takes a long sip. "Well, I think I've probably told you that he cheated?"

I nod. "You've mentioned. But I'm getting the idea there may be more to the story."

"You could say that." He takes a deep breath. "He'd been having an affair with a woman he worked with for years. She got pregnant. He had to choose between our marriage and being part of the baby's life. He chose the baby."

I blink at him. "Holy Christ, I didn't realize. I'm so sorry."

He shrugs, his eyes not meeting mine. "Aren't you going to ask me how I never suspected? How I could possibly not have known what was going on?"

"What?" I ask, confused. "Jesus, of course not! How on earth could you be expected to know something like that?"

He huffs. "Well, that always seems to be the first question anyone asks." His expression softens as he finally meets my gaze. "Thank you. For not assuming I'm either willfully ignorant or as blind as a bat."

I grab his hand from where it rests on the bed. "I'd never think either of those things about you."

He gives me a small smile. "Andrew is a pilot," he begins. "A few years ago, he got an opportunity to relocate to New York. It was a big deal for his career—more routes, better advancement prospects. We talked it over, and I was supportive. I mean, it meant we'd be apart more, but I wasn't willing to leave the West Coast because of my family and my business with Jeff, and I wanted Andrew to succeed too."

I nod, not wanting to interrupt.

"He got a roommate there, a flight attendant he worked with. Ashley." Jesse's jaw tightens. "She was great. I would have even called her a friend. It made sense financially, and I liked that he had some company when he couldn't make it home on his days off. I was fine with the whole thing."

He lets out a bitter laugh. "Turns out I should've been a lot less fine with it, since they started sleeping together almost right away. For years, he lived this double life. When he was in San Diego with me, he played the devoted husband. In New York, he and Ashley were building a life together."

Anger on his behalf surges through me. "God, that's absolutely vile. How did you find out?"

Jesse's eyes meet mine, pain evident in their depths. "She got pregnant. And suddenly, Andrew had to make a choice. Us or them."

"And he chose them," I finish softly.

Jesse nods. "It was the right decision, of course. There was a child involved, after all. But it sucked for me at the time. Although, who the hell knows, if they hadn't gotten pregnant, the whole thing could still be going on, and I might have no idea to this day."

White-hot rage courses through me. *What a bastard.* The urge to unleash a torrent of curses is overwhelming, but I bite my tongue. Instead, I take a deep breath and squeeze Jesse's hand tighter. "I'm so sorry you had to go through that. You didn't deserve any of it."

"Thank you," he says softly. "I know that now, after a few years of intense therapy. But do you know what still messes with me?"

I shake my head. "What?"

He pauses, swirling his wine like a sommelier. "*I knew*. I *knew* right down to my bone marrow that Andrew was my person. But I was *so, so* wrong. And if I was wrong about that, what else am I wrong about?" He shakes his head in frustration.

I nod. "I can understand why you'd see it that way. But you must know that it wasn't your fault. You trusted someone you loved, and he betrayed that trust. That's on him, not you."

"Intellectually, I get it. But actually being able to put myself out there again, to trust that I'm not going to get burned... that's a whole different ball game."

"Jesse," I say, waiting for him to meet my eyes. "I want you to hear this. You are not broken. Don't let that arsehole's actions define the rest of your life." I take a deep breath. "Don't cut yourself off from the possibility of love just because one relationship didn't work out like you thought it would."

Chapter Nine

Jesse

With Martin lying beside me, I sleep better than I have in years. I wake bright and early, ridiculously excited about getting to show Martin the park. Martin's sleeping on his stomach, the sheets shoved down around his waist, and I allow myself a few moments to take in how beautiful his body is in the soft morning light. He might be in his fifties, but the man has clearly taken very good care of himself, because the sight of his strong, muscled back makes my mouth water, and my cock hardens.

"Martin," I whisper, gently shaking his shoulder. "Time to wake up, sleepyhead."

He groans, burrowing deeper into the pillow. "Jesse, it's too early," he mumbles, his accent thicker with sleep. "The mouse can wait."

"But you have to get up! It's time for some magic," I deadpan, teasing my fingertips along his spine.

He cracks open one eye. "Unless you're talking about the magic wand you've got between your legs, I've no plans to leave this bed anytime soon."

I laugh, allowing my hand to drift lower, dipping under the sheet so I can tease his ass. "Okay, well let's make a deal. Come shower with me and I'll let you play with my magic wand there."

He flips over onto his back, the tented sheet giving me a pretty good idea of how much he likes that idea, even as he fixes me with a playful glare. "You know, I can think of a great many magical things we could do that don't involve leaving this bed." He waggles his eyebrows suggestively.

I lean in and tease him with a quick peck on the lips. "Oh, I'm well aware, but if you join me in the shower I promise to make sure you won't regret it."

I laugh again as he reaches for me, but I duck out of his reach, hopping out of bed. "Come on, old man, our day of fun and adventure awaits!"

He sighs dramatically as he swings his legs onto the floor. "Clearly, you've cast some type of spell over me with that magic wand. That's the only reason I'd even consider getting out of bed at this ungodly hour," he grumbles as he follows me into the luxurious bathroom.

"I know, I know," I say soothingly as I turn on the water before wrapping my arms around him. "But I promise, it will all be worth it."

He rolls his eyes as we step under the warm water together, and I make good on my word, making sure he has no regrets about getting out of bed early.

After making our way into Disneyland, I watch Martin's eyes light up at the sight of Sleeping Beauty's Castle.

"Isn't that something," he breathes, shaking his head in wonder.

"Wait until you see it lit up at night," I tell him, squeezing his hand. "It's even more magical then."

We make our way down Main Street, U.S.A., and Martin's head swivels from side to side, trying to take in all the sights and sounds. The smell of freshly baked cinnamon buns wafts from the bakery, mingling with the scent of popcorn from nearby carts.

"You up for a roller coaster this early in the morning?" I grin at him when we approach the Big Thunder Mountain ride.

He hesitates for just a moment before shrugging. "Why not? When in Rome, right?"

We both laugh our asses off as the ride zooms through the herky-jerky twists and turns. Martin whoops with delight at each drop and curve, his hand gripping mine tightly. When we exit the ride, his hair is charmingly disheveled and his cheeks are flushed with excitement.

"That was bloody brilliant!" he exclaims, eyes shining.

We spend the next few hours exploring the different lands, riding all the rides, and generally soaking in the atmosphere. Martin's childlike wonder never fades, and it's completely endearing.

It's afternoon by the time we've seen most of the highlights, but I want to make sure we get plenty of time in what I know will be Martin's favorite part.

"So what do you think, are you ready to take a journey to a galaxy far far away?" I ask with a smile.

I love the excitement dancing in his eyes when he returns my grin. "Lead the way, Captain Solo."

We spend the rest of the day exploring every inch of Galaxy's Edge. His enthusiasm is contagious as we wander through the meticulously crafted streets of Batuu.

"This is incredible," Martin breathes as we stand in line for the Rise of the Resistance ride. His hand finds mine, fingers intertwining. "Thank you for bringing me here."

I squeeze his hand. "I'm so glad you're enjoying it."

"So much," he grins, leaning over and taking my mouth in a sweet kiss.

We spend the rest of the afternoon and long into the evening immersing ourselves in everything *Star Wars.*

I even convince Martin to let me get him one of the custom-made light sabers that lights up, and while he won't admit it, I know he's completely thrilled by the silly souvenir.

By the end of the night we're both exhausted, and I wrap my arm around him, pulling him in close to me as we amble slowly back toward our hotel, full of junk food, candy and some of the best memories I've made in a very long time.

After getting back to our room, we're both exhausted and sweaty from the long day on our feet in the hot sun, so we each take a shower. By some unspoken agreement, we both slide under the cool, crisp sheets of my bed once we've rinsed off the day. He extends his arm, and I snuggle into his warm body, resting my head on his chest, feeling like I'm exactly where I belong.

"So, was I right? Was it worth getting out of bed early?" I ask sleepily.

He chuckles. "It was bloody fantastic, I'll give you that, but please god don't tell me we're getting up early again tomorrow! I'm an old man, I need my rest!"

I laugh, placing a gentle kiss to his pec as I run my fingers through the hair on his abdomen.

"Nope, we hit all the highlights today. Tomorrow we can sleep in and go back to our favorites," I say. "No timeline, no schedule. Just a nice, relaxing day."

"Thank god for small mercies," he chuckles, squeezing me tighter.

We lie together quietly for a few moments, his fingertips tracing gentle patterns on my arm, before he speaks again. "This really was wonderful. Thank you, Jesse. It... It means so much to me. I can't remember the last time I've had as much fun. And it's all because of you."

He looks down at me, and my breath catches at the tender look in his eyes.

"I feel the same way," I whisper softly. "I've always loved this place, but today, being here with you, was special. You made it even better. So thank you."

We share a soft gentle kiss, and my last conscious thoughts are that I always want to fall asleep right here, with my head on Martin's chest and his arms wrapped around me.

Chapter Ten

Jesse

I unlock the front door, my body still humming with excitement from our trip. Martin follows close behind, his presence a warm comfort at my back. As we step inside, the familiar scent of home wraps around us, grounding us back in reality.

"That was an amazing weekend, Jesse," Martin says, a soft smile playing on his lips.

"Yeah," I agree, unable to find the right words myself. The past couple of days feel like a dream, and I'm not quite ready to wake up.

I take our bags upstairs, not even hesitating before placing his bags in my room instead of the guest bedroom. I don't know exactly where things are going to go between us, but I know for sure I want him in my bed and close to me for as long as he wants to be there.

After I get back down to the kitchen, we fall into an easy rhythm as we start preparing dinner. It's as if we've been doing this for years, not just a few weeks. Martin chops vegetables while I season the chicken, stealing glances at him when I think he's not looking.

I reach across to grab the paprika from the cabinet on the other side of where he's standing. My arm brushes against his back, and he leans into my touch, so I linger for a moment longer than necessary.

When I pull back, Martin turns to face me, his pupils blown. Goddamn. For someone in his mid-fifties, he's insatiable. I fucking love it. We're standing close, so instead of thinking too hard about it, I lean in to capture his mouth with mine. He lets out a groan, and his cock hardens against my thigh.

The timer on the oven beeps, startling us both. We both laugh and jump apart, the sexual tension broken, but in its place is a comfortable intimacy.

After we eat, I stack the last plate in the dishwasher and turn to Martin, who's wiping down the counter.

The setting sun fills the kitchen with soft, golden light, and I'm struck by how right this feels.

"Hey, I'm feeling a bit lazy tonight. What do you say we skip our walk and watch *Star Wars* instead?"

Martin's eyes light up. "Sounds perfect. Which one?"

"How about *A New Hope*? Can't go wrong with the classic."

He nods, a grin spreading across his face. "I'll make the popcorn."

While Martin busies himself in the kitchen, I head to the living room and cue up the movie. I settle into the corner of the couch, stretching an arm and a leg along the back.

He joins me a few minutes later, a large bowl of popcorn in his hands. Without hesitation, he sits right between my legs and nestles into me, his back resting against my chest.

As the iconic opening crawl begins, I can't help but marvel at how comfortable I am with all of this. It's only been a few weeks since Martin moved in, but it's like he's always been here. The weight of his body against mine, the scent of his shampoo, the warmth of his skin—it just feels… perfect.

We watch in companionable silence, occasionally reaching for popcorn or commenting on our favorite scenes. When Martin laughs at Han's quips, I feel the vibration in my own chest.

Halfway through the movie, I realize I've been absentmindedly running my fingers through Martin's hair. He lets out a contented sigh, nestling closer.

"This feels nice," he murmurs, his eyes still fixed on the screen.

I hum in agreement, not wanting to break the spell with words. The domesticity of the moment washes over me—us on the couch, *Star Wars* on the TV, the remains of our shared dinner in the kitchen. It's everything I thought I'd lost the chance at having after my divorce.

As the movie ends, Martin yawns before getting up off the couch. He leans back in a decadent-looking stretch, and I can't stop my cock from twitching when he lets out a groan of pleasure.

"Come on," I say, getting to my own feet and extending my hand to him. "Bedtime."

By some unspoken agreement, he follows me into my room instead of heading across the hall to the guest bedroom. Which is exactly what I was hoping for.

We brush our teeth standing side by side, and I'm struck again by how normal this all feels.

I slip into bed, relishing the warmth of his body next to mine. He settles in, his back pressed against my chest, and I drape an arm over his waist. The contentment I feel is almost overwhelming.

Just as I'm about to reach over and turn out the light, my phone buzzes on the nightstand. I groan, reluctant to move, but curiosity gets the better of me.

"Everything okay?" Martin murmurs, his voice already thick with impending sleep.

"Yeah, just a text. Probably Jeff," I reply, grabbing my phone.

Sure enough, it's from my brother. I scan the message quickly, my brow furrowing. "Hmm, looks like I need to head to San Francisco later this week for a meeting with the governor on one of our initiatives."

"Mmph. How long will you be away?" Martin mumbles, pressing even closer into me.

"Just a couple of nights," I say, tossing my phone aside and pressing my body against his.

"Good," he murmurs. "Don't want to be away from you long," he says, and I'm pretty sure he's already asleep when the next words leave his mouth, but they make me feel warm and happy all the same. "You belong with me."

Chapter Eleven

Martin

A few days later, I wake to an empty bed, the sheets still warm from Jesse's body. The sound of his suitcase wheels rolling across the hardwood floor echoes through the house. I pad out to the kitchen, rubbing sleep from my eyes.

"Heading out already?" I ask, my voice still rough with sleep.

Jesse looks up, a soft smile spreading across his face. "Yeah, early flight. Didn't want to wake you."

I lean against the doorframe, drinking in the sight of him. "You know I don't mind."

He crosses the room, pulling me into a tight embrace. I breathe in his scent, committing it to memory.

"I'll be back before you know it," he murmurs against my hair.

I nod, not trusting my voice. As he pulls away, I feel a familiar ache in my chest. It's been years since I've felt this way about anyone.

"Safe travels," I manage to say as he heads for the door.

"I'll talk to you later," he says warmly as he heads out.

I spend the rest of the day feeling unsettled, and I don't like it one bit. There's no reason I should be feeling so out of sorts just because I'm on my own for a few days. For god's sake, I've been on my own for more than twenty years.

But of course, I know that's not the real reason for my off mood. I miss Jesse. The thought sends a jolt of surprise through me. It's absolutely ridiculous. We've been spending so much time together since our weekend at Disneyland, and now, I find myself relying on having him around like I haven't done since Richard. The warmth of his laughter, the way his eyes light up when he talks about things he's passionate about, like the shelter project, even the simple way he moves through a room—it's all become a part of my daily rhythm.

Uncertainty gnaws at me, a persistent itch I can't scratch. A strange sense of dread hangs over me, making me restless. The day drags, and I can't help but wonder how I arrived here. After spending so many years being so very careful to protect my heart, somehow Jesse has woven himself into the fabric of my life in only a few weeks. As I stare out the window, I grapple with a truth that's both terrifying and exhilarating—I have feelings for Jesse that go far beyond what I intended.

Early in the evening I'm standing in the kitchen, trying to decide what to make myself for dinner, when my phone rings. A smile spreads across my face when I see Jesse's name on the screen.

"Hey there, handsome. How's San Francisco treating you?"

"It's good to hear your voice." The warmth in his tone makes my heart skip a beat. "The city's the same as always. Foggy and full of hipsters."

I chuckle, leaning against the counter. "Interesting. How did your day go?"

"It went well, actually. Jeff and I got a lot of prep work done." He pauses, and I can sense something's off.

"What's wrong? You sound tense."

Jesse sighs heavily. "Andrew contacted me."

My stomach drops. "Oh?" I try to keep my voice neutral, but a knot of anxiety forms in my chest.

"Yeah. He... he wants to meet me for dinner tomorrow night after Jeff and I are done with our meeting."

I close my eyes, willing myself to stay calm. "I see. And how do you feel about that?"

He sighs, heavily. "Honestly? I'm not sure. Part of me wants to tell him he needs to fuck right off, but..." He trails off.

"But another part of you needs closure," I finish for him.

"Yeah. I think I might go. Is that... Do you think I should see him?"

The question hangs in the air between us. I want to say no, to beg him not to see Andrew. But that's not fair. "It's not really for me to say, Jesse. You need to do what's right for you."

"I know. But I just... I wanted you to know. To be honest with you."

"Thank you," I say. *I can handle this.* I trust Jesse. Absolutely, I do. It's just that... he was so broken up about the end of his marriage. What if he sees this as a chance to fix everything and get his life back on track?

"Any idea what he wants to talk about?" I ask, not sure if I want the answer.

"No," Jesse sighs noisily. "Who the fuck knows with him."

"Hmm. I wonder what it could be?" I muse. "Maybe he has to tell you that his pecker got chopped off in a tragic lawnmower accident."

Jesse gasps in shock before bursting into laughter, a sound that makes me light up. "Maybe that's it."

I snort a laugh. "Or maybe he has to let you know the airline's transferred him to Antarctica."

Jesse chuckles. "Or maybe he's been demoted to baggage handler, and now he's asking for alimony."

My next words spill out before I can stop them. "Maybe his girlfriend kicked him to the curb and he's going to beg you to take him back." *Dammit.* I hold my breath, waiting for his reaction.

He snorts. "Maybe he's shit out of luck on that one."

I understand what he's getting at, but for some reason my mind fixates on the word "maybe". *Maybe he's shit out of luck... Or maybe he isn't? Jesus fecking Christ, could I be a more pathetic twat?*

"Yeah, what?" Jesse says in a muffled voice, and I realize someone's in the background talking to him. My stomach clenches unpleasantly, until I remember he's staying at his brother's house, and their three college-age kids are home for the summer. I know he loves spending time with them, so I decide to end our conversation so he can get back to his family. And before I say something stupid that makes me look like an insecure fool.

"Listen, love, it sounds like you're busy there. I should let you go. But you have a good night," I say, injecting as much warmth into my voice as I can. "And good luck with the meeting with the Governor tomorrow. You and Jeff will do a bang up job, I'm certain."

"Thank you, Martin." I can hear the smile in his voice. "I, um.. I miss you. Sleep well."

My heart warms, and I tell myself I'm being truly ridiculous to worry. Jesse cares for me. He makes it obvious in every one of our interactions.

"I'm glad you called, Jesse. You sleep well also. We'll talk tomorrow, yeah?"

"Absolutely. Good night."

After ending the call, I stare at the phone in my hand, a mix of emotions swirling inside me. Fear, jealousy, and an overwhelming sense of helplessness.

I know Jesse needs to face his past, but I can't shake the worry that Andrew might be trying to worm his way back into Jesse's life. *And where does that leave me?*

Later that night, I toss and turn in bed, the sheets tangled around my legs. I think back to that night we'd both had trouble sleeping and we bumped into each other in the kitchen. That moment where we almost kissed drove me crazy. I'd had to jerk off as soon as I got beck to my bed, even though he'd gone running out of the kitchen like his ass was on fire.

I keep replaying our conversation tonight about Andrew. My stupid imagination conjures up images of them sitting across from each other at some fancy San Francisco restaurant, reconnecting over a bottle of wine.

What if Andrew apologizes? What if he's changed?

I know Jesse. He's forgiving to a fault. He simply doesn't hold grudges, it's kind of amazing. That's one of the things I lo— *No. Don't even think that word.*

But it's true. Jesse's capacity for forgiveness is beautiful. And terrifying.

My chest tightens as I imagine Jesse listening to Andrew's excuses, his warm brown eyes softening with understanding. Because that's who Jesse is. He sees the best in people, even when they don't deserve it.

I roll onto my back, staring at the ceiling. The room feels big and empty without Jesse here. I've grown used to his presence, his steady breathing beside me at night.

This, right here, is the reason I've been so damn careful to keep my sex life to impersonal hookups only. Because these feelings, these fears crowding my mind right now are acutely painful. Worse than the occasional bout of loneliness. *I fucking hate it.*

What if I lose him?

The thought hits me like a physical blow. I've been here before. The sickening, creeping fear settling into my bones is familiar, even though it's been so long since I've felt it. When Richard was first diagnosed the fear that filled me back then is eerily similar to what I feel now.

My god, I'm going to be all alone. Again.

I've spent more than half my life alone, and just as long telling myself I'm perfectly okay with it.

And now, the second I decide to even think about letting my walls down, the second I allow myself to dream, even for a moment, of a life where I'm not a lone wolf, out here in the world with no one, it gets ripped away.

Richard's loss still aches, a wound that's never fully healed. And if I lose Jesse now... I'm not sure I'll be able to put myself back together again.

I squeeze my eyes shut, willing the thoughts away. *I'm overreacting. I'm being ridiculous.* I know it's true. I'm being silly. But the thoughts won't stop.

What if Jesse decides he made a mistake with me? What if Andrew is his true love, and I'm just... a place-holder?

The fear wraps around me like a cold, damp blanket. I've allowed myself to get too comfortable, too hopeful.

I should have known better.

Chapter Twelve

Jesse

Walking into Il Forchetta, I'm disoriented for a moment, like I've stepped through a portal back in time and the last two and a half years haven't happened. Before we moved to San Diego, this was my favorite restaurant. Andrew never liked it; it wasn't fancy enough for him. Which is why I picked it for tonight's meeting. *Spiteful? Yes. Do I give one single shit? No.*

I spot him at a table in the back.

"Hey," he says softly as I slide into the chair across from him. I have to stop myself from cringing when his eyes rake over me. "You look really good, Jess."

I nod, not sure how to respond. It's been over a year since Andrew and I have been in the same room, and

I'd expected to be hit with a tsunami of pain and regret when I saw him. But instead of pain, I feel, strangely... nothing.

We make stilted, painful conversation about the weather and other stupid crap until our drinks arrive. As soon as the server disappears, Andrew clears his throat and leans forward, his eyes earnest.

"So, um, you're probably wondering what this is about," he starts, and I just nod, wanting nothing more than to get this over with.

"I need to apologize, Jesse. The shit that happened between us—actually, no," he pauses for a second, closes his eyes briefly and sucks in a deep breath. "The shit I did to you—I just want you to know how much I regret it. Truly, from the bottom of my heart, Jesse, I'm so sorry for everything."

I blink at him. This is *not* what I was expecting.

"I know I've said it before," he continues, "but... I'm in therapy now, and, well, I was selfish and stupid and horrible to you, and I just... I need you to know that what happened wasn't ever about you, Jess. It was all on me."

I listen to his words, trying to gauge their sincerity. I've heard Andrew apologize before, but something feels different this time. There's a rawness to his voice, a vulnerability I've never seen in him before.

But I still don't trust him. "What is this about, Andrew? Do you want something from me? Is that it?"

Pain lances across his face, and I cringe inwardly. Even though he's an asshole, I still don't like hurting him. Apparently, I'm not built for revenge. His expression smooths over, and if I didn't know better, I'd swear the color rising in his cheeks is shame.

He takes a deep breath before looking at me again. "Yeah, I deserve that. But no, I don't want anything from you. Other than I just... I need you to know how I feel."

I narrow my eyes at him, trying to see if I can find a motive for whatever this is written on his face. But all I can see is sincerity, and it makes me angry because he's a liar. He's a goddamn liar and I *know* that now, but there's still part of me that thinks he's telling the truth. The fact that my gut is telling me to believe him makes rage bubble up in my chest.

"Why are you doing this? Why now? I don't get it," I grit out through my painfully clenched teeth.

He looks down at the table again and grabs his fork, fiddling with it nervously before answering.

"Well, I'm in therapy now, like I said," he says, still not meeting my eyes. "I want to be a good dad to Emma, and I want her to grow up with a proper family." He pauses again, finally putting down the fork and instead playing a quick game of chess with the salt and pepper shakers. "I need to make this thing work with Ashley. So I need to be a better husband to her than I was to you."

I wait for the pain to slice through me, the white-hot agony of missing him and the life I thought we had together. But it doesn't come. The rage that was bubbling in my chest only moments ago has drained away, replaced by something that feels like... pity.

He really did make a mess of things. He fucked up my life, but he also fucked up his own. And maybe this is a real effort to be a better person.

"Okay," I say slowly. "I guess I can understand that. It's good that you're trying to grow as a person—your daughter deserves that."

Suddenly, I'm hit with an unexpected feeling of peace, and I can see everything as clear as day. I've been blaming myself for not being able to see Andrew for who he truly was. I thought I'd been wrong about him the entire time. But I get it now. I wasn't wrong about him: he's exactly the same person he always was. He's not evil, and he didn't set out with some grand plan to hurt me; he just lost control of his life. I was collateral damage, which sucks, but it's not a reflection of me or my judgment about people.

My instincts are just fine. Love is a leap of faith, no matter who you're in it with. All I can do, all anyone can do, is work every day to make a relationship work and hope the other person does the same.

Suddenly, I realize I've heard everything I need to from Andrew. The weight I've been carrying for months—years, even—lifts off my shoulders. I don't need to sit through the rest of this dinner pretending we're friends or that his words can fix what's broken between us.

"Andrew," I interrupt, my voice steady. "Thank you for this. I appreciate your apology, and I'm glad you're working on yourself. But I need to go."

He blinks, surprise etched across his face. "What? We haven't even ordered yet."

I'm already standing, fishing my wallet out of my pocket. I toss a couple of bills on the table for my drink. "I know, and I'm sorry. But there's somewhere I need to be."

Understanding dawns in his eyes. "You've met someone?"

I pause, a smile tugging at my lips. "Yeah, I have. And I need to tell him something important."

Andrew nods, a mix of emotions playing across his face. "Go. Be happy, Jess. You deserve it."

Without another word, I turn and stride out of the restaurant. The cool night air hits my face, and I feel like I can breathe properly for the first time in years. I pull out my phone, quickly booking the next flight to San Diego.

As I wait for my Uber, my heart races with anticipation. I need to get back to Martin. I need to tell him that I'm not afraid anymore, that I'm all in. That what we have is real and worth fighting for.

Chapter Thirteen

Martin

The night stretches on endlessly, sleep evading me as my thoughts are consumed by Jesse and his ex. As the sun begins to rise, I'm a jumble of nerves and dread. The 'what-ifs' have spun wildly out of control, and I can't escape the feeling that I'm on the verge of losing it all.

Again.

Somehow, I manage to rein in my emotions and force myself to make breakfast. I'm perched at the breakfast bar clutching my coffee when I catch myself trying to decide where to hide the mug for him today—before remembering with a start that he's not here. Our little game isn't going to happen tonight.

But I remind myself that I'm an adult who's been alone for most of his life. Even if my fears do come true and Jesse ends up taking his shitty, lying ex-husband back, I'll be fine. I'll survive because that's what I do. I survived being abandoned by my family when I was only a teenager, I survived losing the love of my life, and I survived as a single person for almost twenty-five years. I'll survive this too.

I push through the day, though it drags relentlessly. I feel as though I'm treading water, just barely keeping my head above the surface, as I wait to hear from Jesse.

I resist the urge to do something reckless, clenching my jaw as the clock ticks on. But come 5:00 p.m., the floodgates open, and I pour myself three generous fingers of whiskey, the amber liquid swirling in the glass like my turbulent thoughts. I flip on the TV to something ridiculous and mindless before collapsing onto the couch in a heap. I know the show isn't going to work to distract me, but I leave it on anyway, blaring annoyingly in the background as I lie there and stew.

Not long after the warmth from the alcohol spreads through me, I surrender to the exhaustion that's been clawing at me all day. I let my eyes drift shut, the world around me fading as the weight of a sleepless night and a day of relentless obsessing finally pulls me under.

I wake up with a start a couple of hours later, my heart pounding in my chest. I grab my phone off the coffee table, desperately hoping for anything from Jesse—some indication that he's coming back to me, that he feels what I feel.

But there's nothing.

Goddammit.

I can't do this. It's too much.

Before I know it, I'm yanking open drawers and closets, throwing clothes haphazardly into my suitcase. My hands shake as I stuff shirts and socks into the bag, not bothering to fold anything.

"Feckin' eejit," I growl at myself. "What were you thinking, getting involved like this?"

I zip up the suitcase with more force than necessary, the sound echoing in the quiet room. *It's better this way. Leave before I get left. Protect what's left of my poor, shriveled little heart.*

But when I reach for my phone to book a flight back to Seattle, Jesse's face appears on my lock screen—a candid shot from our trip to Disneyland. He's laughing, eyes crinkled at the corners and he's looking at me like I'm the most precious thing in the world.

My finger hovers over the screen, unable to do it. I'm not strong enough to cut this off without at least seeing him first. *Goddammit all to hell.*

I collapse onto the side of the bed, holding my head in my hands.

Suddenly, an idea strikes me. Celeste. I look at the clock. Yes, it's late in Montreal, but she's always been a night owl.

With trembling hands, I dial her number. It rings once, twice, and I almost hang up, but then—

"Martin, tu parles d'une belle surprise! How nice to hear from you again so soon!"

"Hi, Celeste," I say, but my voice is strained, and she can tell right away that something's wrong.

"Martin, what is it? Are you ill?" she asks, fear lacing her voice.

"No, no, it's nothing like that. I'm fine," I say, and she breathes a sigh of relief.

"Merci au ciel," she says softly. "Tu m'as fait une p'tite peur."

"I'm sorry, I didn't mean to scare you," I apologize. "I just... I need to talk to someone."

"Don't apologize, mon cher. I'm unfortunately at the age where my mind jumps to the worst possibility. Now, tell me what's bothering you."

"I... I don't know," I admit, my voice cracking. "I think I've gone and done something stupid."

"What is it? What's happened?"

"Jesse, the man I'm working with here... things have changed between us. I... I—"

When I have trouble finishing my thought, she does it for me. "Oh, Martin. You've fallen in love with him, oui?"

"I... I think so. Yes. I have." The realization hits me in the chest. All of my fretting and worrying is far too late. I've already done what I promised myself I would never do. I've fallen in love with Jesse Greenwood.

"But why are you so upset, mon cher? Isn't this a good thing?" Her voice is gentle, and I close my eyes, trying to hold back the tears threatening to spill over.

"I'm so fucking scared I might lose him, Celeste. It's driving me mad. I—he had dinner with his ex-husband tonight. It's late, and I haven't heard from him yet, and all I can think of is that maybe they're going to get back together. I'm just stuck here in his house, waiting for him—waiting for the axe to drop, and I can't take it. I've already packed a bag. I need to leave because I can't—"

"Martin, stop," she says firmly. "You're spiraling, darling. You need to slow down a moment. Take some breaths together with me. "

I hear her take in a deep breath and I do as she asks, mimicking her as she guides me through a few more inhales and exhales until my heart isn't pounding quite so wildly.

After I've managed to calm down some, I'm able to tell her what I'm feeling without sounding like I need to be carted off to an institution.

When I've finished my sad little story, she's quiet for a moment.

"Tell me something, cheri. Has Jesse given you any reason to believe he still has feelings for this man who betrayed him?"

I pause. "No, he hasn't," I admit. "But he's such a kind person, he's so forgiving. He always wants to believe the best of people, Celeste, even the worst people."

I can hear the smile in her voice. "Martin. Do you think there's a chance you are not giving this man enough credit? What is that old saying, 'Do not mistake my kindness for weakness'? Just because he might forgive his ex-husband does not mean he wants to reconcile."

I suck in a deep breath through my nose and blow it out through my mouth, trying to stave off the panic again. I know she's right, but it doesn't stop my fear. "I just can't stop my mind from worrying that he's going to come back and tell me it's over between us. And the most ridiculous thing is, we haven't even defined what we are to each other! But, god, Celeste, I... I really love him. I haven't even told him, but I can't deny it."

To my shock, Celeste lets out a small laugh. It's a bit watery-sounding, and then she sniffles.

My stomach tightens. "Are you... Celeste, are you crying?"

She laughs again and the tinkling, joyful sound is much more like her. "Only a little, my dear, Martin. It's just that I'm so happy for you. I have been waiting so long to hear you say those words. To know that you're finally, *finally* ready to open your heart again."

What? Hasn't she been hearing me? "But... I just... I don't think I can survive losing someone I love again. I'm not strong enough. I... I can't do it..."

"Oh, Martin," she sighs. "You are so much stronger than you give yourself credit for. I understand your fears—that's natural. But I think you've protected yourself *too* well. For all these years you've avoided getting hurt, yes, but you've also avoided any real happiness." She pauses. "And, mon trésor, Richard would be devastated if he knew."

Her words hit me like a gut punch. I know she's right. Richard would be horrified if he knew about all the years I've spent alone, carefully avoiding any kind of meaningful attachment.

"You have so much love inside you, Martin. And you've buried it for much too long. Please, darling, please don't hide it again. You're a man who is built to love and be loved. That sounds silly, and—what's the word in English—corny? But even so, I believe it is true. You are a loving person. You need to share that love."

I'm stunned at her words. Celeste and I have always been close, but we've never had this kind of no-holds-barred conversation.

"Give your Jesse a chance," she continues. "You must stop fear from stealing any more of your life. You can still be afraid, but you need to be brave. It's been too many years already of letting it control your life."

I sit with that for a moment. "I don't know. I just... I don't know. Maybe I can try."

"*I* know," she says, her voice firm with confidence I don't share. "I know you can. Now, promise me you'll wait and talk to him. Don't run."

I take another deep breath. *Fucking hell.* I don't know what I expected to hear from her, but it certainly wasn't this. I nod, more for myself, since she can't see me. "Okay. I'll try. I promise."

"Good," she says, and I can hear the smile in her voice. "And Martin?"

"Yes?"

"Call me again soon. I want to hear all about this Jesse of yours."

"I will. Thank you, Celeste. I... thank you for everything."

"I love you, my sweet Martin. After all these years, it's time to let yourself live again. Richard would be so proud of you."

My eyes fill with tears as I end the call, and I sit on the edge of the bed for a long time, trying to sort through my feelings, while my packed suitcase sits on the bed beside me.

The overwhelming panic has receded slightly, but I'm still worried. Celeste believes I'm strong enough to deal with whatever comes, but I'm not so sure. All of my instincts are pushing me to flee, to protect the little piece of my heart that's still intact.

I *want* to believe Jesse could feel the same way about me that I do about him. I *want to believe* I'm brave enough to take the risk, to lay it all on the line and trust that will work out. I *want to believe* that I could let myself enjoy a life with him without being constantly afraid that it could all be taken from me in one second.

But I'm not sure I'm as brave as Celeste thinks I am.

I just don't know if I can do this again.

Finally, I decide on a compromise of sorts. I'll keep my suitcase packed and ready. That way, if Jesse does break things off when he gets home, I won't have to torture myself trying to grab things to leave, I'll be able to walk out with at least a little dignity intact.

Maybe it's not the most brilliant plan, but it at least helps me feel less like I'm sitting around waiting for the other shoe to drop.

Chapter Fourteen

Jesse

I burst through the front door, my heart pounding with excitement. It's late, but I couldn't wait. I decided instead of calling or texting, I'd surprise Martin by just showing up and telling him what I realized tonight. "Martin!" I call out, unable to contain the joy bubbling up in my chest. "Martin, where are you? I need to talk to you!"

My eyes scan the living room, searching for him. That's when I see it. A packed suitcase sitting by the door.

The words die in my throat. My stomach drops. *What the hell is going on here?*

"Martin?" I call again, more hesitantly.

He appears from the hallway, his face a mix of emotions I can't read.

"Hi," he says, and his expression is unreadable.

I can't take my eyes off the bag. "What's... what is this? What's going on? Are you leaving?"

Martin follows my gaze, then looks back at me. He runs a hand through his hair, a gesture I've come to recognize as a sign of nervousness. "I... I don't know. Maybe. I was thinking about it."

"Thinking about it?" My voice is weirdly high pitched. "What the hell? *Why?*"

He takes a deep breath. "I just assumed, Jesse. Your dinner with Andrew, and I didn't hear from you... I started thinking about all the ways this could go wrong."

I step closer to him, my heart aching. "Martin, I—"

"No, let me finish," he interrupts. "I've been so happy these past few weeks. Happier than I've been in years. And it's bloody terrifying. Because the last time I felt this way..."

"Richard," I finish for him.

He nods, his eyes glistening. "I don't know if I can go through that again, Jesse. I don't know if I'm strong enough."

I want to pull him into my arms, to tell him everything I realized during my dinner with Andrew. But I'm frozen, suddenly second-guessing everything I'd been so sure about only a few minutes ago.

I stare at Martin, my mind racing. He's packed his bags. He's ready to leave. Maybe I was wrong; maybe he doesn't feel the same way about me that I do about him. I want to grab him, pull him into me, hold him tight and tell him everything I feel.

But the crushing doubt has me paralyzed. Again. *Maybe he needs space. Maybe I pushed too hard.*

"Martin," I start, my voice wavering, "I... I didn't know you felt this way. I thought..." *Jesus fuck.* I stand there gaping at him, mute with shock at how incredibly badly this is going.

Everything seemed perfectly clear during dinner. And then, I spent the entire flight home imagining this amazing, romantic scene. I'd rush in the door, Martin would be thrilled to see me, we'd kiss, and I'd tell him all the things figured out. I'd tell him how much I love him, and how I've been letting all my stupid insecurities hold me back. I'd tell him that even though it seems fast, it doesn't matter, because I'm old enough to know what I want. And I want him. Forever. And just like that, we'd go on to live happily ever after. Or something like that.

Maybe I had it all wrong. Again.

His eyes widen slightly as I stand there, gawping at him like a fish, and a flash of something—hurt?—crosses his face before he quickly masks it.

"Maybe some space from each other would be best." His voice is low, and he shifts his gaze away from me, down to the suitcase sitting on the floor.

I want to scream that it's not what I want. That he can't go, because I love him, but the words stick in my throat.

Martin shifts his weight. "Maybe we rushed things," he says, his gaze skittering from his suitcase to the door and back again, looking anywhere but at me. "Maybe we need to take a step back." His voice sounds so far away.

I'm speechless, and the walls feel like they're closing in on me. *I don't understand. How did we get here?* My brain struggles to compute what's happening.

"I'll be in touch about the shelter," he says softly before picking up his suitcase and walking out the door.

The click of it closing behind him echoes through the empty house.

I have no idea how long I stand there, stuck dumb by my old friend, decision paralysis. But then I see a car pull up, and I watch as Martin starts to load his small bag into it, and something inside me snaps. *Finally.*

"What in the *fuck* am I doing?" I mutter, nearly ripping my front door off its hinges.. He's not leaving without hearing me out. If he wants to leave after that, fine, I can't control that. But I'm not going to just stand around and let it happen. I've been doing that for my entire life, and I'm fucking done. I am just *done* with letting life simply happen to me. Starting right now, I'm fighting for what I want. And what I want is the man who's getting into the back of a car, about to drive away from me.

"Wait!" I shout, racing across my front yard as fast as my legs will move.

I grab the car door, wrenching it back open just as Martin's about to close it. Without a second thought, I launch myself into the back seat, crawling onto his lap. His eyes widen in shock, but I don't give him a chance to react. I cradle his face in both hands, my thumbs brushing over his cheekbones.

"Jesse, what—" Martin starts, but I cut him off.

"No! Shut up and listen to me," I bark, my voice surprisingly firm. "You don't get to walk away like this. Not without hearing what I have to say."

His hands come to rest on my hips, steadying me. His touch sends a jolt through my body, reminding me of all the reasons I can't let him go.

"I love you," I declare, my heart pounding so hard I can barely hear my own words. "I love you, and I'm not letting you leave because you're scared. I'm scared too, but I know what I want now. I want you."

His eyes search mine, a mix of hope and fear swirling in their depths. "Jesse, I—"

"No, let me finish," I insist, my thumbs still caressing his face. "I know you're afraid of losing me like you

lost Richard. But Martin, I'm right here. I promise
you I will be here for as long as the universe will let me.
I'm not going anywhere. And I want to spend every
day proving to you how much I love you.

I pause, catching my breath, my eyes never leaving
his. The tension in the car is palpable, and I'm suddenly aware of the driver watching us in the rearview
mirror.

"Look," I continue, lowering my voice, "No one
knows how much time we have left. No one can
promise they'll be together for the next hundred years,
because we don't know if we get a hundred years. It
could all be over tomorrow for me or for you, or for
everyone on this planet, for all we know. But, *fuck*,
isn't it better to spend the time we do have with the
person we love? That's what I want, Martin. I spent
all this time doubting myself. Telling myself that the
things I knew about you couldn't possibly be true,
that I couldn't be sure. But I was wrong because I've
known ever since that night in Seattle. I love you. And
I want to spend every fucking day that I have left on
this Earth with you. I want to build something with
you. A life. A love. The shelter. A family. All of it. I

want everything I can get with you. And I won't give up. I'll never give up. I'll fight for you as long as I need to." My chest is heaving as the words pour out of me like water from a faucet.

Martin's hands tighten on my hips, and I feel a surge of hope. "Jesse," he starts, his voice rough with emotion, "What if—"

"What if nothing," I interrupt, shaking my head. "You know what I realized while I was sitting across from my ex-husband tonight? I realized that I'd be a fucking idiot to let this chance go. Sure, I loved Andrew once upon a time, and it didn't work out how I wanted. You loved Richard and it didn't work out how you wanted. So, what, we're just supposed to give up now? No! No way, fuck that." I press my forehead to his. "We've both been around long enough to know how rare this thing between us is. I refuse to let you walk away because you're scared, that's not a good enough reason. What we have is real. I feel it. You feel it. I'm done letting fear control my life, Martin. You should be, too."

Martin's breath hitches, and I place one of my hands on his chest, where his heart is slamming against his ribcage. "What if something happens to you?" he whispers, his vulnerability laid bare. "I don't know if I can bear losing someone I love again."

My heart swells.. He loves me too. "We can't predict the future," I say softly, brushing away a tear that's escaped down his cheek. "But I'd rather spend whatever time we have together than waste it being afraid."

I can see the battle raging within him as our eyes lock. Fear and hope are duking it out inside his heart as I hold my breath.

Finally, a small smile tugs at the corners of his mouth. "I love you too," he says, his voice barely above a whisper. "I can't fight it anymore. I love you so fecking much." His Irish accent is as strong as I've ever heard it.

I crush my mouth onto his, pouring every ounce of love I can into the kiss. His lips part beneath mine, and I deepen the kiss. Martin's hands slide up my back, pulling me closer, and I lose myself in the feeling of his body against mine. This perfect man that I love. He's mine.

Time stands still. The world fades away, and all that exists is Martin and me, here in this moment. I never want it to end.

Reality crashes back in when the driver clears his throat. Loudly.

I jump back, suddenly remembering where we are. Heat floods my cheeks as I meet the driver's amused gaze in the rearview mirror.

"Sorry," I mumble, but I can't keep the grin off my face.

The driver shakes his head, giving me a sunny smile. "Don't worry about it. This'll make a great story for Reddit later: 'Y'all won't believe what happened in my back seat today...'"

All three of us burst out laughing, the tension in the car dissipating.

"Well," I say, still perched on Martin's lap, "I guess we should probably get out of your car now, huh?"

The driver winks at us. "Unless you two lovebirds want me to take you somewhere?"

I grin down at Martin. "You going anywhere, my love?"

"Never," he says, his green eyes twinkling. "Never again."

Epilogue

Six Months Later

Jesse

I shift in my seat as the Uber weaves through the late afternoon traffic, my knee bouncing with a mix of exhaustion and excitement. After a grueling week of meetings, I'm finally headed home to Encinitas—and more importantly, to Martin. I can't wait to see him.

Digging my phone out of my pocket, I quickly tap out a text.

> Me: Just left the airport. Be home soon, love.

His reply is almost instantaneous, making me smile.

> Martin: Just drop your bags at home and meet me at Moonlight instead.

I raise an eyebrow, my curiosity piqued. Moonlight Beach is still our favorite spot, the place we take our nightly walks together to watch the sun dip below the horizon in a blaze of oranges and reds.

> Me: Everything okay?

> Martin: Everything's perfect. Just thought we could take an evening stroll before heading back. I've missed you.

A warmth blooms in my chest. God, I've missed him too—his laugh, his sarcasm, the way his eyes crinkle when he smiles. This past week apart has seemed long. It's the longest we've been apart from each other since we officially decided to be together six months ago.

> Me: Sounds amazing. I'll see you soon.

Pocketing my phone, I lean back and gaze out the window, watching the familiar sights pass by. My body may be drained from long flights and endless meetings, but my heart is light with anticipation of seeing my love.

These last six months of living together have been the happiest of my life. After the pain of my divorce and the initial fear of opening myself up again, Martin helped me rediscover joy, passion, and the courage to love wholeheartedly. He's become my safe harbor, my best friend, my everything.

I can't wait to see him.

After a short pit-stop at the house so I can ditch my suitcase inside, the Uber pulls up along the beachfront, and I quickly thank my driver before hopping out. The salty ocean breeze caresses my face as I start down the path.

My eyes immediately find Martin sitting on our favorite rock, just beside the main lifeguard office. The setting sun bathes him in a warm, golden glow, as he gazes out at the endless waves rolling in, and my breath catches at how beautiful he looks.

As if sensing my presence, he turns and meets my stare. A slow smile spreads across his face, crinkling those laugh lines I love so much. Rising from the bench, he opens his arms to me.

I break into a jog, the week's tension melting away with each step.

I pull him flush against me, breathing him in—that warm, earthy scent that's uniquely his. "God, I missed you so much," I murmur into the crook of his neck, my lips brushing his skin.

He shivers in my embrace. "Not half as much as I missed you, love." His fingers thread through my hair, sending tingles down my spine.

We stand there for endless moments, just holding each other close, our hearts beating in sync. The crashing of the waves fades into the background as I lose myself in the solidity of his arms around me, the comforting familiarity of his touch.

After so many years of closing myself off, of putting up walls to guard my battered heart, Martin broke through every one of my defenses. He saw me at my most vulnerable and loved me anyway. With him, I don't have to hide or pretend - I can simply be myself, flaws and all.

Pulling back, I gaze into those warm brown eyes that never fail to take my breath away. "I love you," I whisper, meaning it with every fiber of my being. "You've made me happier than I ever dreamed possible."

Martin's eyes shine with tenderness and a hint of mischief. "I love you too, mo ghrá." His lips quirk. "But as much as I'd love to ravish you right here on this beach, I've a surprise first."

He chuckles at my raised eyebrow and extracts himself from my arms. Taking my hand, he tugs me further down the shore. "Come on, you."

I follow him, curiosity bubbling inside me. He pulls me toward an outcropping of rocks jutting out from the cliffside which create a small alcove, sheltered from the wind. I stop in my tracks, my breath catching at the sight before me.

"What is all this?" I whisper, awe coloring my voice.

He's transformed the secluded patch of sand into a magical oasis. A plush beach blanket is spread out, inviting us to sink into its softness. Surrounding it are wooden posts stuck into the sand, draped with twinkling fairy lights that cast a warm, ethereal glow over everything.

A small Bluetooth speaker plays soft jazz, the mellow tones drifting on the ocean breeze. The centerpiece of this enchanted setting is a wicker picnic basket.

He tugs me toward the blanket, a shy smile playing on his lips. "I wanted to welcome you home properly."

We settle onto the blanket, and Martin begins unpacking the basket. He pulls out a bottle of my favorite Cabernet Sauvignon, two stemless wine glasses, and an array of mouthwatering goodies.

There's a charcuterie board laden with an assortment of cured meats, artisanal cheeses, and dried fruit. Crusty bread and crackers accompany olives and sun-dried tomatoes. My stomach growls appreciatively.

"And for dessert, we have your favorite truffles from that little shop downtown," he says, producing a small box of gourmet chocolates.

I'm overwhelmed by his thoughtfulness. This man, who once convinced himself he was too set in his ways for love, has created the most romantic setting I've ever seen.

"Martin, this is... incredible," I manage, my voice thick with emotion. "I love it. Thank you."

He reaches out, cupping my cheek in his hand. "You're worth every bit of effort."

A while later, I lean back against his chest, savoring the warmth of his body and the gentle rise and fall of his breathing. I'm pleasantly full and relaxed. The wine has left a pleasant buzz humming through my veins, making everything feel soft and dreamy. The sun has long since dipped below the horizon, leaving us bathed in the soft glow of the fairy lights. It's like we're in our own private universe, the two of us wrapped up in a cocoon of contentment.

His fingers trace lazy patterns along my arm as we listen to the waves roll in. The rhythmic sound blends with the soft jazz still playing from the speaker, and I simply can't imagine a more perfect moment.

"Jesse," he murmurs, his breath warm against my ear. "These past six months have been the best of my life, you know."

I turn to look up at him, my heart swelling at the emotion I see in his eyes. "For me too," I agree, reaching up to brush my fingers along his jawline.

He catches my hand, pressing a kiss to my palm. "I never thought I'd have this again," he continues, his voice thick. "After Richard... I convinced myself I was done with love. That I was too old, too set in my ways."

I stay quiet, giving him space to gather his thoughts. Martin's not usually one for grand declarations, so I can tell this means a lot to him.

"But you," he says, shaking his head with a soft laugh. "You came crashing into my life like a bloody hurricane. Turned everything upside down in the best possible way."

"Careful," I tease gently. "You're dangerously close to being romantic."

He rolls his eyes, but his smile is fond. "Cheeky bastard," he mutters, before his expression turns serious again. "I mean it, Jess. You make me happier than I ever thought I could be again. I love you so fecking much."

My heart skips a beat as he gently nudges me to lean forward. I shift, curious and a little confused, until he reaches into his back pocket. Time seems to slow as he pulls out a small velvet box, and suddenly, I can't breathe.

Martin's eyes, usually so confident and full of mischief, are wide with vulnerability. His Adam's apple bobs as he swallows hard while he shifts onto one knee in front of me.

"Jesse," he begins, his voice uncharacteristically shaky. "I never thought I'd be doing this again. But you... you've changed everything for me."

I'm frozen, my mind racing to catch up with what's happening. Is this real? Is Martin really about to...?

He takes a deep breath, steadying himself. "You've shown me it's never too late for love, that my heart still has room to grow. You've become my home, my safe harbor, my greatest adventure."

Martin opens the velvet box, revealing a simple, elegant platinum band. The fairy lights dance off its polished surface, and I feel tears prick at the corners of my eyes.

"Jesse Greenwood," Martin continues, his voice growing stronger even as it trembles with emotion. "Would you do me the incredible honor of becoming my husband?"

The world narrows to just this moment - the soft sand beneath us, the gentle crash of waves, the twinkling lights, and Martin's earnest, hopeful face. My heart feels like it might burst.

Martin

My heart pounds against my ribs like a wild animal trying to escape its cage. Sweat beads on my forehead despite the cool ocean breeze, and my palms are so clammy I have to wipe them on my jeans. I can barely breathe as I watch Jesse's face.

My legs tremble, and I'm grateful I'm already on one knee. If I were standing, I might collapse from the sheer intensity of this moment. The ring box in my hand feels impossibly heavy, as if it contains all my hopes and dreams for our future together.

"Yes," Jesse breathes, his voice thick with emotion. "God, yes, Martin. Of course yes!."

My heart explodes with joy. I surge to my feet, nearly dropping the ring in my rush to rip it out of the box and put it on his finger. Jesse's arms are around me in an instant, crushing me against his chest. I bury my face in his neck, inhaling his scent as tears of happiness stream down my cheeks.

His body shakes against mine, and I realize he's crying too. But when I pull back to look at him, he's grinning so wide I'm concerned his face might split right apart. A laugh bubbles up from my chest.

"I love you," I choke out. "So feckin' much. Christ on a bike, look what you do to me!"

Jesse laughs, and cups my face in his hands, his thumbs brushing away my tears even as his own continue to fall. "I love you too, Marty-love. More than I ever thought possible."

I gaze at this man. This love of my life, his face radiant with joy, and I'm struck by how far I've come. Only one year ago, I was convinced I'd spend the rest of my life alone, clinging to Richard's memory like a lifeline. But now, here I am, engaged to this incredible man who's brought light back into my world.

It took me a while to learn it, but Jesse, together with some help from Celeste, helped me truly understand that loving him doesn't diminish the love I had for Richard. In fact, it's the exact opposite: it honors that love.

I can almost hear Richard's voice, teasing me for taking so long to open my heart again. He'd be thrilled to see me now - happy, in love, building a future with someone who cherishes me.

I can barely contain my excitement as we hastily gather up our things and pack away the trash from our romantic dinner. We stumble across the sand, giggling and stealing kisses like lovesick teenagers as my heart races, desire coursing through my veins.

We practically sprint home, our hunger for each other thick in the air. I fumble with the house keys when we reach the front door as he ghosts his hot breath across the back of my neck. My cock surges to attention in my pants, making it nearly impossible to focus on the damn door lock.

Finally, the door swings open. We tumble inside, dropping our beach gear unceremoniously on the floor. Before I can catch my breath, Jesse pushes me up against the door, his body pressing into mine.

"God, I need you," he growls, grinding his hips against me.

I moan, my head falling back against the door as his lips find my throat. My fingers tangle in his hair, pulling him closer, and his hard length presses into my leg, ramping up my desperation for him.

He slides his hands under my shirt, splays his fingers across my back, and pulls me more tightly against him. My breath catches. There's almost nothing hotter than when Jesse gets desperate and feral like this.

With a fierce growl, he lifts me off my feet, pressing me harder against the door, so I wrap my legs around his waist. His taste drives me half mad and his tongue tangles with mine, stroking and teasing and sending shivers down my spine. My head spins and my body begs for more as we press into each other, every gasp and moan spinning us up even higher.

I thread my hands through his hair, holding onto him like I'll never let him go—because I don't plan to.

He teases the skin just above the waistband of my jeans with his fingertips, and I rock my hips against him in search of more friction.

My heart is galloping, my skin on fire. With a sharp tug, I put just enough distance between us to yank his shirt over his head, breaking kiss just long enough to admire his gorgeous, bare chest. But then his lips are on my neck, his teeth grazing my pulse point right above my own t-shirt, and I rasp out a low groan.

His mouth travels downward, lips and teeth grazing my collarbone. My head falls back, letting out another wanton moan. All I can do is cling to him, my fingers digging into his muscled back, trying to pull him even closer.

"You feel so damn good," he murmurs, his voice husky and filled with need. His hands slide lower, cupping my ass and hitching me higher against him.

He bends his head to tease my nipples through the material of my shirt, biting and nipping at them until I'm a writhing, panting mess.

"Jesse," I groan, my voice hoarse with need. "Bedroom. Now."

With one last scorching kiss, he tears himself away and sets me down, his eyes dark with desire. My legs are wobbly, but somehow I manage to stay upright as he grabs my hand and pulls me up the stairs to our room.

A familiar thrill sparks in my chest as we stumble to our bed, both ripping off our remaining clothes as we go. God, I love surrendering control to this man.

He pushes me onto the bed, and I sink into the mattress, my heart racing as he hovers over me, his eyes burning with raw desire. With another low growl, he captures my lips, kissing me deeply.

His mouth is demanding, possessing, and I can't get enough. I slide my hands over his broad shoulders, down the strong muscles of his back as I arch into him. I moan into his mouth, my body burning everywhere we touch.

He trails kisses down my neck, and I let out a whimper. When Jesse's like this, so controlling and fierce, I'm nothing but putty in his hands, powerless to resist as he explores my body with his lips and tongue. It's by far the most sensual, arousing, erotic thing I've ever experienced. The physical chemistry we share is some-

thing I've never known, and I'm completely addicted to it.

His mouth continues its scorching path, leaving
me breathless and begging for more. Each touch
sends more shocks of pleasure through me, and
what little control I had left slips away. I'm his
to command, and surrendering everything to him
thrills me like nothing else.

"God, Jesse," I gasp as his lips find a particularly
sensitive spot on my neck. "I need—"

"I know what you need," he growls, his eyes glit-
tering.

My words are gone at this point. My senses are
overwhelmed, my body alive with sensation. His
bites and kisses brand me, claiming me for everyone to see. My world narrows to his touch as I let
the outside world go and my entire focus is Jesse:
his taste, his scent, the sound of his ragged breath
mingling with mine.

Sitting back on his heels, he runs his palms over
my thighs, teasingly close to where I ache for him.
His eyes are dark and his touch is electric, sending
sparks throughout my entire body.

He teases me, brushing my cock ever so lightly with the tips of his fingers. I gasp, and then groan painfully as he gives me a wicked smile. He knows exactly what he's doing, his soft, feather-like touches causing my hips to jerk involuntarily. I'm almost thrashing on the bed by now, but still, he merely teases, his touch maddeningly light, as he relishes my torment. God, the man knows how to make me beg.

"You're so beautiful," he murmurs before leaning back over me and running his tongue along my collarbone, his breath hot against my skin. "I could look at you forever."

I whimper again, desire pooling in my gut. "Jesse, please—"

My words turn into a sharp gasp as he shifts down my body suddenly, and quickly envelops my cockhead with the searing, wet heat of his mouth. Sensations explode through me, white-hot and electrifying. My back arches, my hips thrusting involuntarily.

A deep groan rumbles in his throat, the vibrations nearly sending me over the edge. I grab his hair, desperately needing to ground myself, even as I thrust roughly into his mouth, unable to hold back for even one more second.

Jesse's tongue swirls and flicks, driving me wild. My breath comes in short, sharp pants.

I close my eyes, unable to bear the erotic sight of his mouth stretched wide around my girth. Every muscle in my body is taut, coiled tightly like a spring ready to snap.

His mouth is scorching, his tongue a slick weapon as he works me over relentlessly. I can't think, can't breathe. I'm on fire, every nerve ending screaming for release as he takes me impossibly deeper, his cheeks hollowing out as he sucks hard. A strangled cry tears from my throat, my hips jerking helplessly.

And suddenly, right as I'm teetering on that knife-edge of release, he pulls off me. I let out a frustrated roar, snapping my eyes open to see that wicked glint in his eyes and an evil grin on his face.

"No. No! Please, please, Jesse," I beg shamelessly, but he just runs his palms slowly over my heaving chest, a smug smile on his lips.

"So eager," he murmurs, his voice thick and husky. His dark eyes never leave mine as he slowly and deliberately reaches to the nightstand for the lube, and just as slowly opens it and pours a generous amount onto his fingers.

Then, with a smirk, he pours a slick trail down my crack, making me shiver.

His touch is feathery light as he begins to tease me open, circling my entrance but not pressing inside. I groan, as he taunts and teases me.

"Please," I beg again, my voice hoarse. "Jesse, I need—"

He silences me with a deep, searing kiss, stealing my breath at the same time as he pushes one finger gently inside me.

A shudder runs through me at the intrusion, that pleasure-pain that makes my toes curl.

He breaks the kiss, his eyes dark and hooded as he sits back to watch his finger slide in and out of me. "You good?" he whispers.

"Yes," I hiss, my hips moving to meet his rhythm. " I need more."

Jesse takes pity on me, sliding a second finger inside me . He stretches me slowly, carefully, his gaze never leaving mine.

I clench around his fingers, and he chuckles darkly. "So damn tight, my love. God, you feel so good, Martin."

His words send a rush of heat through me. I love the way he says my name, the way he makes me feel wanted and cherished. I can't take my eyes off him as he prepares me, his fingers working gently but relentlessly.

"Jesse, please. I need you. Now."

He freezes, his eyes searching mine, as if confirming I'm sure. And I am. God, I am.

With a growl, he pulls his fingers out and lines his cock up with my hole. I hold the backs of my thighs, opening myself to him. My chest heaving with desire and anticipation of the pleasure I know is coming.

I feel the head of his cock at my entrance, and let out a slow, deep breath as he pushes inside my eager body.

We both groan as I take him in, and I shudder when his thighs press up against my ass as he gets fully seated. He falls forward onto me, our bodies fully fused together in every way they can. He rotates his hips, and I can feel him deeply inside me. I let out a sigh as happiness courses through me. We're exactly where we should be. This man was made for me. My body knows this as surely as it knows how to breathe. I look deeply into his eyes as our breaths mingle. I move so I can hold his face between my palms.

"God, I love you, Jesse. I love you so much." My voice breaks, and inexplicably I feel my eyes fill. Jesse and I have made love before, but this... This feels transcendent.

"I love you, Martin. More than I've ever loved anyone. Ever," he breathes out, his expression is raw as he moves inside me. "God, you feel so... I can't describe—"

"I know baby, I feel it too," I whisper as I reach up to press our mouths together. He wraps his arms around my head as he holds me close, only breaking our kiss to breathe.

Our bodies move together like we're one being, each of us knowing instinctively what the other needs. Slowly, what began as slow and infinitely gentle becomes faster and harder, but our connection, the intimacy only grows stronger as we stare into each other's eyes.

As our movements pick up speed, the room is filled with our soft gasps and sighs, murmurs of love flowing between us easily and without thought. the sound of our love and our passion filling the room.

We're both approaching the edge of our orgasms. Jesse's smooth thrusts start to stutter and he has to close his eyes for a moment. "Martin, I can't, I'm so close," he chokes out.

"Do it, come with me now, love. Now!" I shout as my own orgasm crests, my body tightening around him as he squeezes his eyes shut and thrusts into me hard, every muscle in his beautiful body tensing as he empties inside me at exactly the same moment I release, my orgasm lasting for what seems like forever.

He collapses onto me, our bodies slick with sweat, both of us gasping for breath. I hold him against me, not wanting to release him from my body, wishing he could simply stay in me forever.

He nuzzles into the crook of my neck as we come down from our high. I feel his heart hammering in his chest almost as clearly as I feel my own. His breath is warm across my sweaty skin as I run my fingertips gently through the sweaty tendrils of his hair at the base of his neck, savoring this perfect, dreamy afterglow.

Finally, our breathing slows to a steady rhythm, and our heartrates return to normal. His cock softens, and we both wince as he slides out of me.

"I love you so much, he says with a sweet smile, and my regular, gentle-natured Jesse is back. I love the way he gets feral and commanding during sex sometimes, but when Jesse is just being Jesse, he's pretty fucking amazing as well.

"I love you, too, my husband-to-be," I say with a grin as he moves to lie beside me, gathering me into his arms and pressing a kiss into my temple.

We share a chuckle as we lie tangled together. The silence stretches between us, comfortable and intimate. The peace I feel when we're together this way feeds my soul unlike anything else can.

Loving Jesse hasn't been easy every day. As with every relationship, there are plenty of ups and downs. Sometimes my fear that something will take him away from me gets out of control. And there are times Jesse still struggles with self-doubt.

But we both know that no matter what the future holds, we'll be there for each other, for as long as the universe will let us. We're willing to take that leap of faith that is love, again and again, for as long as we both shall live.

Thanks for reading Love After Love!

I hope you enjoyed Jesse & Martin's story! If you want more sweet, steamy MM romance from Harper Robson, check out From The Ground Up. (Book 1 of the Hot Dam Homes series) on Amazon and in Kindle Unlimited

https://mybook.to/fromthegroundup

Curious about how Penn & Harper got together? Check out Making Waves for their story. Available at https://mybook.to/makingwaves

How About Steamy M/M Hockey Romance with ALL the Feels?

Check Out the *Seattle Sasquatch Series*
Book 1: Rylan is available NOW!
https://mybook.to/rylan

Rylan

One hot night with my teammate threatens to expose my secret and end my career.

I've spent my entire hockey career hiding who I really am. Between trying to lead my struggling team, dealing with an alcoholic father, and living in the shadow of my brother's legacy, my life feels like one endless fight. The last thing I need is for anyone to discover my secret. Then Jamie Pirelli arrives—young, talented, and openly queer. He sees through all my walls, and suddenly everything I've built is at risk.

Jamie

I'm more than just the first openly bisexual player in the league.

After a disastrous start to my pro hockey career in Florida, Seattle is my last chance. I can't afford any more scandals, but the chemistry between me and my deep-in-the-closet captain is impossible to ignore. Our connection on the ice is what hockey legends are made of.

Off the ice... is a different game altogether.

Rylan is a high-stakes hockey romance between the team captain with loads of baggage and the younger superstar struggling to be taken seriously. An impossible-to-resist forbidden relationship between a wounded control freak with a tragic backstory and a sunshiny free spirit with a tarnished reputation.

Also By Harper Robson

The Hot Dam Homes Series

From The Ground Up: Mason & Jackson https://
mybook.to/fromthegroundup

When The Walls Come Down: Dylan & Reed htt
ps://mybook.to/whenthewallscomedown

Built To Last: Tyler & Sam https://mybook.to/bu
ilttolast

Part of the *Hot Dam Homes* World

A Clean Slate(Available for free at www.harperrobs
on.com)

***An Unexpected Gift: A Hot Dam Homes Christ-
mas Novella https://mybook.to/anunexpectedgi
ft***

The Getaways Series

Making Waves: Hunter & Penn https://mybook.t
o/makingwaves

Making Waves Audiobook: Narrated by Kevin
Earlywine & Cole Michael Kurcz
available at shop.harperrobson.com

Love After Love: Martin & Jesse (a Getaways Novella) https://mybook.to/loveafterlove

The Seattle Sasquatch Series

Rylan: Book One https://mybook.to/rylan

Louis: Book Two (2025) https://mybook.to/lou

Austin: Book Three (2025)

Carson: Book Four (2026)

Part of the *Seattle Sasquatch* World

The Night Before: Aleks & Ben https://mybook.to
/thenightbefore

A *Seattle Sasquatch Hockey* Christmas Prequel Novel

All books are available on Amazon and in Kindle Unlimited (unless otherwise noted)

All About Harper Robson

Harper Robson grew up dreaming about being a writer someday. That someday didn't arrive until she was in her mid-forties–but better late than never! While traveling that long and winding road, she worked in marketing, software development, the oil & gas industry and spent more than a decade as a stay-home mom. She grew up in Vancouver, BC, but feels most at home in the leafy green suburbs of Seattle, Washington. In 2023, Harper and her clan pulled up stakes and headed south to live in San Diego, California. She was certain she'd miss the rainy, gray days of the Pacific Northwest, but it turns out regular doses of sunshine and palm trees are pretty easy to get used to, and San Diego feels more like home every day.

She's a mom to two teenaged boys and an adorable but naughty yellow Labrador Retriever. Her husband works in the tech industry and he makes her laugh every single day.

A true PNW girl, Harper loves the rain but is always planning her next beach vacation. Her favorite things include road trips, classic rock, the Seattle Kraken, her dogs, and drinking champagne for no reason at all.

She would love to hear from you anytime! Email her at harper@harperrobson.com

Visit harperrobson.com and sign up for the Newsletter

Let's Connect!

The best way to keep up with all things Harper is to sign up for the VIP Newsletter: https://www.subscribepage.com/harpernewsletter

―――ℓℓ―――

Bluesky: @harperrobsonauthor.bsky.social

Facebook: Harper Robson

Instagram: @harperrobsonauthor

BookBub: @harperrobsonauthor

Facebook Group: Harper's Heartbreak-ers: https://www.facebook.com/groups/harpersheartbreakers

―――ℓℓ―――

Goodreads:

https://www.goodreads.com/author/show/2228446

9.Harper_Robson

Amazon Author Page

https://www.amazon.com/author/harperrobson

Website: www.harperrobson.com

Get Your Free Book!

A Clean Slate

Head over to

www.subscribepage.com/harperbackmatter

to sign up for my VIP newsletter. You'll receive a free copy of *A Clean Slate,* Eric and Drew's steamy, age-gap love story.

Eric

I've been dealing with a chronic illness since I was nine years old, and, believe me, it's a drag. Being a Type 1 diabetic affects every relationship in my life, from my parents all the way through the guys I date. After getting unceremoniously dumped because of it,

I've decided that romantic relationships aren't in the cards for me. The last thing I want is to be a burden on anyone. But when my best friend drags me to a weekend memorial for his grandmother and I meet his uncle, I start to wonder if he means it when he tells me I could never be a burden.

Drew

Being a single, gay man in New York city and making a decent living as a writer isn't a bad gig. But after the end of a long-term relationship, I'm at a crossroads. I can stay here and continue on with life as I know it, or I can take this opportunity to make a big change and start over in a new place. I've spent my entire adult life resisting change, but when I travel across the country for my mother's memorial weekend, I meet someone who makes me think that jumping in with both feet might not be the worst decision. The problem is, he's my nephew's best friend, and he's half my age.

A Clean Slate is a steamy, age-gap romance featuring a New York City-based writer and a West Coast

Ph.D student who probably shouldn't fit together, but somehow do.